"Nothing

"Please, Marcie, let me in ... ... in everything." Giving up on the doorbell, Sam started pounding on the door.

Part of her wanted to do as he asked. The wronged woman in her wouldn't let her.

"Maybe you noticed your clothes are in the hall," she pointed out. "You and I are through."

At first he didn't believe she was serious. "You're mad at me and I don't blame you," he soothed. "But I spent the night at Jack's."

Hope surged in Marcie's heart. They'd had a fight, that's all. She could slide back the bolt and let Sam take her in his arms.

Childhood memories stayed her hand. Her father's lies, her mother's tears.

Well, she wasn't going to be such an easy target.

"I've put up with a lot, Sam. But this was the last straw. If you give me your new address, you'll be hearing from my attorney!"

Suzanne Carey is a former reporter and magazine editor who prefers to write romance novels because they add to the sum total of love in the world.

Recent titles by the same author:

DAD GALAHAD

THE
MALE ANIMAL

BY

SUZANNE CAREY

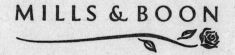

MILLS & BOON

All the characters in this book have no existence outside the imagination of the author, and have no relation whatsoever to anyone bearing the same name or names. They are not even distantly inspired by any individual known or unknown to the author, and all the incidents are pure invention.

MILLS & BOON and the Rose Device
are trademarks of the publisher.
Harlequin Mills & Boon Limited,
Eton House, 18-24 Paradise Road, Richmond, Surrey, TW9 1SR

© Verna Carey 1994

ISBN 0 263 79392 3

Set in Times Roman 10 on 12pt
91-9602-54890 C

Made and printed in Great Britain

I WENT THROUGH ALL THIS PAIN FOR HER CAUSE SHE
LIKED **FLOWERS** — NOW SHE WONT SPEAK TO ME!
TO TOP IT OFF, THESE ARE PERENNIALS!

Chapter One

September, 1992

Where was Sam, anyway? It was getting late. He'd need time to shower and change if he didn't want to arrive at the banquet looking and smelling like a pair of dirty sweat socks.

Smiling sweetly as she offered Des Whitney a refill of his gin and tonic and another smoked-trout canapé from her favorite midtown caterer, Marcie couldn't help wishing that, for once, her husband of three years had skipped his usual late-afternoon sojourn at the Golden Gloves Gym and the inevitable bull session that followed it at Flannery's Bar.

Though he drew his popular syndicated cartoon strip, "Male Animal," at their apartment, Sam was always gone by the time she arrived home from work. For the most part she didn't complain, though sometimes she wanted to. She knew that the boxers and trainers with whom he rubbed elbows on a daily basis provided him with a wealth of material for his strip.

Tonight was different. She'd been notified unofficially a week earlier that she'd receive the prestigious Marguerite Kemp Award for Feature Writing. Didn't he understand how important it was to her?

The situation was particularly trying because of Des. Not that he was at fault in any way. It was just that he, she and Sam were scheduled to attend the awards banquet together. She didn't feel she could suggest hailing a cab and leaving Sam to catch up with them later if he chose.

In town for the convention at which she expected to receive her prize, Des was managing editor of the Charleston, South Carolina, *Gazette,* the family-owned newspaper published by Sam's genteel but high-powered widowed mother, Dacinda St. Martin Jeffords. He was also Sam's third cousin—in an excellent position to report trouble in paradise.

Nodding and smiling in response to one of Des's mildly amusing newsroom stories, Marcie crossed shapely legs beneath the abbreviated hem of her pale yellow jersey cocktail dress and tried not to glance at her watch too much. She wanted to gossip with her colleagues and luxuriate in anticipation, not walk in late and harried partway through dinner. Or miss the featured speaker's opening remarks. The latter scenario was all too likely if Sam didn't come home within the next few minutes.

Though it was uppermost in her mind, getting to the banquet on time wasn't the only thing bothering her. Recently she'd begun to worry about the state of her marriage in general, a much more serious affair. From a cocoon of pure bliss in its early stages, lately her union with Sam had deteriorated into a tug-of-war between opposites.

Life in New York was one of their biggest friction points. A city kid who wrote for *Vanity Fair*'s up-and-coming rival, *Zoom* magazine, Marcie loved the Big Apple, whereas Sam, a relatively recent transplant, had grown to hate it. Critical of the city's frenetic tempo, cramped living conditions and perpetually snarled traffic, he rhapsodized ever more wistfully about South Carolina's marshland and beaches, the easier pace of life in his native Low Country.

He'd move back in a minute if I'd say the word, she realized. Well, there's no way I'd even consider it. My job's tied to living here. Sam knew that when we got married. He can draw his cartoon anyplace. Sighing, she ran absent fingers through her short red curls.

Under no compunction not to raise the subject of Sam's tardiness, Des consulted his Timex. "I wonder what's keeping our fair-haired boy," he said. "He'd better get a move on if he's coming with us."

As if released from bondage, Marcie leapt to her feet. "Maybe I ought to give him a call," she suggested.

The barkeep at Flannery's recognized her voice before she could state her business. "Sam ain't here," he barked.

She *had* been phoning there fairly often of late. "Any idea what time he left?" she asked.

"Ten, fifteen minutes ago."

To her relief, Sam's key turned in the lock as the barkeep slammed down the receiver. Handsome and undeniably sexy in the compact, dark-haired way she liked so much, he was wearing sweat-stained jogging clothes and needed a shave. His manner was decidedly mellow as he shook hands with Des.

It was painfully clear to Marcie, if not to Des, that he'd had one too many beers. Why, oh why, does he have to be so irresponsible? she thought. It's as if he wants to punish me for doing well. "Shall I fix you a cup of coffee while you shower, sweetheart?" she asked.

Stung by what he guessed was a none-too-subtle attempt to control him, Sam pretended not to hear. "I'll be ready in two shakes, guys," he promised, disappearing into the apartment's bed-and-bath area.

At the Waldorf, where the convention was being held, dinner began without a hitch. Determined to enjoy herself after a harrowing crosstown taxi ride, Marcie tried to ignore the less-than-tasteful jokes Sam was telling a female editorial writer at their table. What she didn't hear couldn't hurt her, she supposed. Keeping her back partly turned to them, she focused on a three-way conversation between herself, Des Whitney and Glenn Bokaw, her boss at *Zoom*. It was only when a gap in the conversation coincided with Sam's delivery of a particularly crude punch line that a flush crept into her cheeks.

Things went from bad to worse when a waiter paused to refill her wineglass. Reaching across her for the butter dish, Sam promptly spilled the glass's contents—a white Chablis—on her dress and then helped spread the stain by scrubbing at it with his napkin.

"Sam...don't!" she cried, attempting to evade his ministrations.

To his credit, Sam was thoroughly apologetic. "Sorry, Red," he told her contritely. "If the cleaners can't fix it, I'll buy you a better one. Uh...maybe it's time I headed for the little boys' room."

On his way back from the lavatory, Sam slipped on a scrap of lettuce that had fallen to the parquet floor. Damn! he thought. If I fall, Marcie's going to have my neck.

In an effort to regain his balance, he bumped into a waiter laden with a tray of whipped-cream-topped desserts. The collision sent the desserts flying. Most of the whipped cream landed—*splat*—on the ample bosom of a peau-de-soie-clad matron. She let out a startled shriek.

With a frothy blob highlighting the most prominent feature of her anatomy, the matron looked as if she'd bumped into a cloud. Des whispered as much.

Not to be outdone, Glenn shook his head. "Bunch of dwarves," he drawled. "Lathered with shaving cream."

The mental image was hilarious. To Marcie's dismay, the matron was a publishing bigwig who happened to be on the prize committee. She didn't know whether to laugh hysterically or cry bitter tears.

A Marx Brothers-type comedy skit ensued as several waiters converged in an attempt to help. Finally, they'd done all they could. The damage partially concealed by a neck scarf, the woman returned to her seat at the head table. Marcie prayed she wouldn't notice Sam was her dinner partner when the prizes were handed out.

With little to do but hold down a chair and toy with his unused dessert spoon, Sam managed to stay out of trouble during the guest speaker's address. At last the awards portion of the program got under way. Soon Marcie was hearing the words she'd dreamed about.

"As many of you know, the coveted Marguerite Kemp Award is given each year, not for a single achievement, but for a body of work that richly illuminates contemporary American life," the master of ceremonies announced. "This year, it goes to a young woman who has amply proven her insight and talent for asking the right question in addition to employing an astonishingly vivid, yet lucid, writing style.

"The judges were extremely impressed by her two-part report on the psychology of top politicians, as well as her compassionate, yet candid, interviews with ghetto residents, hurricane victims and women with AIDS. She handles lighter subjects equally well. I know many of you read and enjoyed her effervescent profile of that nonagenarian queen of American theater, actress Lilah Fontaine. Without further ado, ladies and gentlmen of the pen ... or perhaps I should say the computer ... I give you this year's winner ... Marcie McKenna of *Zoom* magazine!''

By now, the wine stain on Marcie's skirt had dried and all but disappeared.

More intimidated by all the praise being heaped on her head than she'd have dreamed possible a few hours earlier, she stood and made her way to the front of the room. The applause was deafening. To her surprise and chagrin, however, when the master of ceremonies motioned for quiet, one member of the audience kept right on clapping. It was Sam, of course. He didn't subside until Des poked him in the ribs.

He gave a repeat performance when, certificate and check in hand and a graceful acceptance speech under her belt, she returned to their table. To make matters worse, he topped it off with a big, sloppy kiss.

''Waiter!'' he cried. ''Where's a waiter? We want some *champagne* at this table. It's not every day a man's wife creams the competition.''

The reference to ''cream'' was an unfortunate one, given his earlier mishap. Besides, in Marcie's opinion, the last thing he needed was another drink. It can't be those beers he had that are causing all the trouble, she thought. His system would have absorbed them long ago. He must have drunk more wine than I realized.

Touched though she was by his obvious pride in her, she was getting awfully exasperated with him. ''Sam, please ... let's just have coffee instead,'' she suggested, aware she probably sounded like a broken record. "I want to hear the closing remarks."

A short time later, the formal meeting broke up and a musical combo started to play. Marcie stood, intent on heading to the rest room to repair her makeup. Promptly following suit, Sam asked her to dance. "You're so smart and pretty. I'm crazy about you," he whispered, pulling her into his arms and nibbling affectionately on her ear.

Hating herself, but uncomfortably aware of the way people were whispering about them, she disengaged herself from his clutches. "I don't want to dance right now," she said. "The way things have been going, you'd probably stumble all over my feet."

By now, Sam believed, he was as sober as a judge. Well, almost. Maybe it was the antihistamine he'd taken so he wouldn't sneeze during the awards ceremony that was making him feel so woozy. More hurt by Marcie's opinion than he was willing to admit, he decided to show her a thing or two. That little brunette at the next table didn't appear to have an escort....

By the time Marcie returned from the rest room, Sam and the brunette were on the dance floor, plastered cheek to cheek. And that wasn't all. Thanks to the popularity of "Male Animal" and its running commentary on relations between the sexes, Sam was hot copy. Seeing his chance for something more exciting than the traditional "awards-ceremony shot," a newspaper photographer assigned to cover the event snapped half a dozen frames of them together.

Marcie was mortified. The previous week, Sam's strip had focused on the varied temptations married men face. Wherever she'd gone, people had teased her about it. She couldn't get them to believe she wasn't his "Redhead" character. Or shake their conviction that the situations he portrayed were drawn from life events. Now he was giving them a firsthand demonstration. More notoriety was the very last thing she wanted.

"Take it easy," Des advised as she slammed her evening bag down on the table. "Sam loves you. It's everyone's prerogative to behave like an idiot now and then."

Marcie did her best not to turn on him. "You think I'm being too hard on him, don't you?" she asked as she slid into her chair.

"Maybe just a little."

"He's made an utter mess of the evening. Try and disabuse me of that."

"I'm afraid I can't."

As one dance tune followed another, Sam showed no inclination to rejoin them at the table. Finally, at Marcie's urging, they approached him and his partner during a pause in the music. "If you don't mind, Sam," Marcie said curtly, "I'd like to leave."

Still smarting over what he considered her condescending manner, Sam dug in his heels. "Fine with me," he replied with a shrug. "Personally, I'm not ready to go yet."

Giving every impression of being a carefree bachelor with no angry wife to placate as the band segued into a slow number, he swept the brunette back into his arms.

By now, Marcie was on the verge of tears. Even Des looked pained. When she asked him to escort her home, he didn't argue. Though he appeared to hesitate, he agreed to come in for a while when they reached her apartment.

Putting the teakettle on to heat, Marcie joined him in the living room. She was aching to unburden herself to someone. But she didn't want her remarks passed on to Sam. Or his mother. Certainly not his sisters and other relatives. As a fellow journalist, Des ought to be able to keep a confidence.

"Can our conversation be off-the-record?" she asked.

To agree meant he wouldn't reveal a word. "All right," he said.

Leaning toward Des over the coffee table, Marcie spilled her guts. Sam hated New York. He didn't like her friends. The fact that she'd kept her maiden name. Or her mother, who'd just divorced again and gone to live in Europe for a while.

He also criticized her failure to cook for him in the manner he'd expected. He complained incessantly about the amount of money she blew on clothes, though she earned every penny of it herself and he was pulling down a six-figure salary. Last but not least, he wanted to start a family—right away.

"Don't you want children, Marcie?" Des asked gently.

Instantly she was on the defensive. "Of course I do! I'm . . . just not ready. My career's not at the point where I can afford to leave it yet."

"I should think with the Kemp Prize under your belt..." Apparently having second thoughts about expressing a personal opinion in the matter, Des left the remainder of his statement dangling.

Unwilling to point out that getting pregnant wasn't such a hot idea if your marriage was in trouble, Marcie wasn't sure how to answer him. She was saved by the teakettle's piercing whistle.

When she returned to the living room with two mugs of instant coffee on a tray, he asked about her complaints instead. Marcie made a face. They were a litany. For starters, she was upset about the way Sam portrayed her in his strip. His slovenly ways. The amount of time he spent with his bachelor buddies. His unorthodox behavior in public drove her up a wall, if Des wanted the truth. He'd witnessed an example of it for himself.

To her somewhat gloomy satisfaction, he admitted it hadn't been the best. But he added, "None of what you've told me seems insurmountable if the two of you are willing to work at things. Don't you love Sam? It seemed to me, when I attended your wedding, that's how you felt."

Tears welled up in Marcie's eyes despite her effort to suppress them. "Oh, Des." She faltered, her lower lip quivering. "You know I do. And you're right.... Most of our complaints do seem petty. But he's out with that brunette someplace! Doing God knows what! If he sleeps with her..."

Sighing, Des joined her on the couch and put a brotherly arm around her shoulders. "In my opinion, Sam's grandstanding to get your attention," he said. "He'll be back...sorry as hell...without having done anything to end a marriage about. Mark my words."

Marcie wished she could be as confident. Whatever the case, she didn't think she could stand to sit around the apartment by herself, waiting up for him.

"Stay until Sam comes home," she begged. "I won't jump all over him if you'll promise to talk some sense to him."

Though Des hung around for a while, and did his best to reassure her, Sam didn't show. Ultimately Des had to return to his hotel. He was scheduled to fly back to Charleston first thing in the morning. He needed rest.

"I know it looks bad for Sam, staying out this late," he acknowledged, giving Marcie a comforting squeeze when she clung to him at the door. "But there's bound to be a perfectly logical explanation. No...*not* the one you think. And I doubt he's been in an accident. Why don't you go to bed and try to get some sleep yourself? God knows, you probably need it. By the time you wake up, Sam will have returned, suitably penitent."

Skeptical, Marcie followed his prescription without much success. After several hours spent tossing, turning and dozing in fits and starts, she awoke fully at some small, indeterminate sound to become painfully aware that she was still alone in the apartment. Sam was asleep somewhere in the city... with the brunette beside him, unless she missed her guess.

The mental image was like a dagger in her chest. Oh, she doubted he'd done the woman much damage, given his inebriated state. But it was the thought that counted. Whether or not it had led anywhere, the idea that he'd let another woman touch him intimately made her want to weep.

The morning paper was probably lying on the doorstep. In an effort to distract herself while she waited to have it out with Sam, Marcie put on a robe and padded out to the hall to retrieve it. Turning to Sam's cartoon first, she winced. Jake, his most prominent male character, was complaining to his health-club buddies about his wife's extravagance. He referred to her as "the Redhead" in case anyone who knew them would miss the point.

"She claims she pinches pennies," he told his buddies in the final frame after citing a lengthy list of purchases. "The trouble is, she pinches them so hard, they jump right out of her fingers."

Frowning at what she considered a personal slam, Marcie exploded when she turned to the paper's "celebrity" section. There, prominently displayed, was a photo of Sam dancing with the anonymous brunette. The accompanying cutlines offered a tongue-in-cheek account of his singular performance at the banquet.

An unaccustomed oath escaping her lips, Marcie flung the paper down on the coffee table. The force of her action overturned Des's coffee mug from the night before, causing the dregs it contained to drip onto the carpet. Humiliated and furious, she didn't bother to blot them up. It was morning and he wasn't home *yet*. She wanted to wring his damn-fool neck!

He simply wasn't going to get away with this. With the steely resolve of a general preparing for battle, she gathered some plastic garbage bags and made a beeline for Sam's half of their walk-in closet and dressing area. Grimly she scooped briefs and socks from his drawers by the handful, cramming them into the bags every which way along with suits, ties and blue jeans, his leather jacket and tennis shoes.

At least he won't have to walk around naked, though his paramour might prefer it, she thought wrathfully as she thrust the bags out in the hall and stepped back into the apartment, slamming the door and locking it. Seconds later, she realized Sam had almost certainly taken his key. He'd put his stuff back the moment he returned—and bawl her out for making such a mess.

Shoving the deadbolt into place solved that problem for the moment. Unfortunately, he'd have renewed access the minute she had to go out. He'd probably lock *her* out in turn. She'd have to call a locksmith, and soon—preferably before he got up from his bed of iniquity and crawled home like the snake he was.

It was too early yet. Tense over the finality of her plan of action and her almost paranoid fear Sam would come home before she could carry it out, Marcie got back under the covers. How huge the bed felt without him in it. And how tragic to think he wouldn't make love to her there again. Their sex life hadn't been that terrific lately, thanks to all the arguments. But it was a lot better than doing without him altogether. She'd never be able to find a man she loved as much.

Once a cad, always a cad. Unbidden, the words surfaced in her head. She remembered her mother saying them about her father shortly before their divorce, when she was eleven. Meanwhile, her burst of adrenaline was waning. Setting the alarm just in case, though she doubted she'd get any sleep, she shut tear-swollen eyes.

The alarm was ringing. Or was it a buzz saw, whining on some nearby construction site? Wearily Marcie fought her way up from the bottom of a well, where she'd been having unpleasant dreams.

"Marcie!" It was Sam. Giving up on the doorbell, he started pounding. "C'mon, babe...please! I know I behaved like a jerk. But nothing happened. I swear it. Let me come in and explain."

Part of her wanted to do as he asked. The wronged woman in her wouldn't let her. Wrapping her robe around her, she went to stand on the opposite side of the door from him.

"Maybe you noticed...your clothes are in the hall," she pointed out. "If I were you, I'd find someplace else to put them. You and I are through."

At first, he didn't believe she was serious. "You're mad at me and I don't blame you," he soothed, his voice taking on a cajoling note. "But it's true what I said. That brunette and I parted company at the banquet. I spent the night on Jack Donovan's couch."

Hope surged in Marcie's heart. They'd had a fight, that's all. Their differences could be mended. She could slide back the bolt and let Sam take her in his arms.

Childhood memories stayed her hand. The conversation as fresh in her mind as if it had taken place the day before, she remembered her father offering her mother a similar excuse. Unfortunately, the detective Elizabeth McKenna had hired to follow him had told a different story.

Of course Sam would say he hadn't gone to the woman's home, let alone slept with her. He'd probably asked Jack Donovan to lie for him. Well, she wasn't going to be such an easy target.

"I've put up with a lot. But I won't have a husband who sleeps around," she told him angrily. "If you'll see that I get your new address, you'll be hearing from my attorney."

Chapter Two

June, 1994—the present

It was almost quitting time. Slouching a little in her orthopedically correct computer chair at *Zoom* magazine, Marcie gazed out the window at the flock of fleecy white clouds that were grazing above the buildings across the street. It was the kind of evening for meeting a man you loved for cocktails and watching the sunset with him afterward from a private roof garden overlooking the East River.

But Marcie didn't have a man in her life. Nor did she possess a roof garden. She wasn't thinking about such things. Instead, she was mulling over a phone call she'd received earlier that afternoon from her attorney, Bob Richmond.

The call had been in the nature of a friendly reminder that time was running out on the temporary legal separation agreement she and Sam had hammered out twenty-one months earlier. Following the lockout episode, Sam had demanded a divorce. Coming partway to her senses, Marcie had authorized Bob to propose counseling. To her surprise, Sam had refused. He'd responded through Jerry Bartholomew, his attorney, that he was cutting his losses. To put it bluntly, he was dumping her *and New York*—moving back to South Carolina where he belonged. Four years in the big city and three years of married life had been enough.

At Marcie's urging, Bob and Jerry had compromised on the separation as a kind of lengthy "cooling-off period," with divorce proceedings to follow if she and Sam failed to resume cohabitation within two years. Sam had okayed the agreement without an argument. To Marcie's knowledge, he hadn't offered any comment.

Choosing his words with care, Bob had asked Marcie how she wanted to proceed. "I haven't heard a thing from Jerry Bartholomew," he'd said. "Sam hasn't gotten in touch with you, I suppose?"

Marcie had been forced to admit he hadn't.

"Well, we should be hearing from Jerry soon." Bob had paused delicately, as if he sensed his client had mixed emotions. "When he does, what do you want me to tell him?" he'd asked.

Her heart heavy, despite the two-year battle she'd waged to get Sam out of her system, Marcie had promised to give the matter some thought. She couldn't seem to get her mind to focus on the practicalities of the matter, though. Instead, as she sipped absently at a mug of cold coffee and stared at the sky, she was remembering how she and Sam had met, at a boxing match she'd covered for *Zoom*. He'd been entranced to find her at such an event. Falling head over heels in love, they'd gotten married much too precipitously.

Looking back, their life together had sometimes been hell, but more often heaven. She still had strong feelings for him. Whenever she let herself think about it, she missed him like a physical ache. She had a deep if irrational sense that, if she allowed the divorce to go through without a fight, she'd lose the best thing that had ever happened to her.

What's the matter with you? she chastised herself. The marriage has been dead for almost two years. It's time to hold the funeral and move on to new possibilities.

Her thoughts scattered when her boss, Glenn Bokaw, stepped into her office. "How's it going?" he asked.

She shrugged. "Pretty well. The piece you wanted on high-powered political wives is in the hopper. I've made a few calls on the research two-parter. But it's slow going. Nobody at Harvard or the National Institute of Health wants to talk."

Natty in a blue blazer and conservative striped tie, the sandy-haired former navy officer grinned at her. "I finished reading the political wives' story a few minutes ago," he said. "It's dynamite."

"I'm glad you like it." Her pensive mood notwithstanding, Marcie couldn't help smiling in return.

"So..." Glenn picked up a paperweight from her desk and turned it over, casually inspecting it. "I don't suppose you saw the blurb in this morning's *Times* about feminist backlash against your husband's comic strip."

Bracing herself, Marcie admitted she hadn't.

It seemed Sam had been egged a few days earlier when he'd given the commencement address and accepted an honorary degree at a small private women's college in upstate South Carolina. In addition to the coeds who'd pelted Sam, a group of National Organization of Women protesters had turned up with placards. There'd been some angry epithets.

Unable to stop herself, Marcie flinched. For some reason, she still felt Sam's exploits reflected on her—that she was obligated to defend him and lead him from the path of error, almost in the same breath.

In what at first blush seemed a non sequitur, though she doubted it, Glenn told her to forget the research story for a while. "It'll keep," he said. "There's something else I'd like you to do first."

All she'd heard that day was "Sam, Sam, Sam." She hoped her new assignment wasn't connected with him.

To her chagrin, it was. "I want you to interview Sam...get his side of the situation," Glenn said. "Talk to the women in his life...find out how they feel about the way he portrays their sex.

"While you're at it, check out his Edisto Island project to save loggerhead sea turtles. That's a side of him most people don't know about. Balance the piece by tracking the column for a couple of weeks and getting some feminist quotes.

"Take a lot of pictures. Sam at the drawing board. Sam with his turtles. Sam and whoever's lighting up his life these days..."

Marcie was violently shaking her head. "No, Glenn... *please!*" she exclaimed when finally he paused for breath. "That wouldn't be objective journalism. I'm his ex-wife, for God's sake."

Glenn usually abided by a "hands-off" policy where her private life was concerned. But he could be fairly direct when he chose. "Not yet, you aren't," he reminded, "though I agree...it does appear your marriage is over."

Though the finality of his comment hit her where it hurt, Marcie was determined not to lose her cool. Or get in an argument with him. She took a deep breath. "All the more reason, then," she said, "to assign the story to someone else."

On the verge of retiring from a second successful career, Glenn knew just when to turn on the charm. "Try to see things my way," he cajoled. "You and Sam are adults. You don't hate each other. Besides, you're a professional journalist, capable of interviewing anyone. You can inform the reader of your connection with him and set it aside. Among the female writers I know, particularly those with feminist leanings, you'd probably give him the fairest shake. You'd never fail to include his good points."

Marcie remained incredulous. "Even if I were willing to do what you suggest, Sam would never agree to it," she said. "Since our separation, we haven't spoken to each other. I don't even have his number."

Glenn didn't bat an eyelash. "Not a problem," he replied, tossing a scrap of notepaper on her desk. "The top number is his Charleston house. The other's his place on Edisto. Give him a call. That's a direct order from your captain, sailor."

Reluctantly dialing Sam's Charleston number after Glenn had left the room, Marcie got his answering machine. Hearing his lazy baritone again, even via a recording, was like a kick in the solar plexus. In a panic, she chickened out and didn't leave a message.

That night, at her Upper East Side apartment—smaller and neater than the one she'd shared with Sam—she checked out her estranged husband's daily cartoon strip. Though any amusement she derived from it was tainted with unresolved feelings from the past, it was something she still did with regularity. Each time, memories crowded in on her. Many of them were irritating. Some were unbearably sweet.

In that day's strip, the married, divorced and single buddies whose misadventures Sam chronicled were seated in a bar very much like Flannery's, discussing the evidence that there were domestic difficulties in heaven, too. "Whadd'ya mean the angels ain't got problems?" his Jake character pronounced with typical disdain for anyone who disagreed with him. "Look at all the bad weather we've been havin' lately. Nothin' but floods, tornadoes and hurricanes!"

In South Carolina, Sam had just returned to Charleston in a dust-covered Jeep from his digs on Edisto, a nearby but appealingly remote, Spanish-moss-draped sea island populated mostly by the descendents of African slaves and—on weekends—tourists and local beachgoers. Since splitting up with Marcie, he'd acquired a "single-house" in Charleston's historic district and a run-down cottage at the edge of a marsh on Edisto, where he labored to save the eggs of endangered loggerhead sea turtles during the spring and summer months.

If I hadn't become a cartoonist, I'd have pursued a career in environmental science, he thought, as he turned into his private, walled courtyard and switched off the engine. Of course, I wouldn't have the bank balance I have today. Or, possibly, the necessary freedom to make a difference.

His house was a classic of its type—three stories of weathered brick and exquisite Greek-revival architectural detail. As was customary for the genre, its narrow side was turned toward the street and ornamented with a false door that opened onto the piazza rather than leading directly indoors. A zone of privacy where Sam spent very little time, the wide, columned piazza faced a garden that looked as if it could use some tending.

One of these days, he was going to landscape the garden. Have the bricks sandblasted. And paint the trim. First, though, he ought to clean out the refrigerator. Maybe do a little dusting. It was high time he got rid of the mismatched odds and ends that had come with the property and did some decorating.

He wondered why he couldn't seem to get moving with those tasks. In an odd way, he supposed, his life mirrored the house. Like his projects, it was essentially on hold. Cluttered with this and that, it was also empty to a large extent.

Enough, already, he thought as he unlocked the front door. Too much introspection is bad for the soul, not to mention the stomach. Dropping his rucksack of dirty clothes in the hall with the idea of sorting and washing them later, he strolled into the kitchen, popped open a beer and placed a frozen care package of she-crab soup prepared by Salome Gibbs, his mother's housekeeper, in the microwave.

These days, he didn't drink much. Two beers was his limit. He had his act together. Yet as he sat at the kitchen table to eat the soup along with some crackers from a tin, his loneliness was an almost tangible thing. Sure, there were any number of women he could call to help him alleviate it. But none who really cared about what he was doing with the loggerheads. Or wanted to share it with him. Most were fixated on his fame, his bank account, the social prominence of his Charleston relatives.

Marcie was different. The Redhead's a thoroughgoing New Yorker, he thought. And I mean that in a positive sense. Success, in the form of achievement, and recognition for it, means the earth to her. But she doesn't give a damn about fame for its own sake. Or covet somebody else's money.

When they'd met, she'd wanted his company, difficult as he'd found that to believe. To *talk* to him. Sometimes to listen. To kiss and make love as if tomorrow would never come. God, how they'd loved each other in the early days. It was enough to fire his gut, remembering.

I wonder what she's doing tonight, he reflected, rinsing the soup bowl and stacking it beside the sink with Monday's dirty dishes. Whether she plans to let the divorce go through. I wonder if she's seeing anyone.

Just then, the phone rang. With a grimace of displeasure at having his ruminations interrupted, he picked up the receiver.

"Jeffords," he grunted.

"Hi, Sam," Marcie's voice said.

Its sweetness cut him like a hot knife slicing through butter. She's calling about the divorce, he thought helplessly. Hoping I won't raise a fuss.

"Hello, yourself," he answered. "What's new?"

There was a slight pause, as if she were weighing the best way to tackle him. "You're not going to believe this," she said at last. "But Glenn wants *me* to do a story on you. I told him you wouldn't agree to an interview. He said to call you anyway."

About to turn her down flat, Sam gave the idea another chance. "What kind of story?" he asked.

"One about you. Your family. The strip. The way you deal with female resentment of the feelings your characters express. Plus your work with the loggerheads. Nobody's paid any attention to that."

Glenn must have held a gun to her head. Or she wouldn't have called. Yet what could it hurt to see her again, if only to put "Paid" to their relationship? At least he wouldn't have to be concerned about fairness. He'd been cut to ribbons by reporters anxious to capitalize on the feminist backlash he'd stirred up. A thoroughgoing professional, Marcie would fashion a more balanced portrait.

He couldn't deny that her interest in the loggerheads pleased him. "I guess it would be all right," he said at last. "When do you want to do it?"

For a moment, she didn't answer him. He'd managed to shock her, he supposed. But then, hadn't he always? Though they'd spent a couple of years apart, she ought to be used to it.

When she spoke, she had herself under control. "How about Thursday?" she asked. "I shouldn't have any problem booking a flight."

He'd be seeing her day after tomorrow. Was he asleep and dreaming this? "Thursday's fine," he answered. "Bring some old clothes, if you have any. I'll take you out to Edisto. If we're lucky, you might get to see one of my oceangoing buddies lay her eggs."

Replacing the receiver in its cradle as if it were made of glass, Marcie hugged herself. Where did we go wrong? she wondered. Things were so special between us once. On the phone, Sam had sounded like a stranger.

Whatever he was to her now, she'd be seeing him in a few days. Gazing into lake-blue eyes that had always seemed able to read her thoughts and fighting the attraction his compact, muscular physique never failed to exert. What if she fell for him again, and he didn't give a damn about her? Supposing he was in love with someone else, and couldn't wait for the divorce to become final so he could marry her?

I'll bet that's it, despite the way he disparages matrimony as an institution, she thought, deliberately torturing herself. He's cooperating so I won't give him any trouble. Her emotions so close to the surface that, if she scratched herself, they'd bleed all over her, she almost jumped out of her chair when the phone rang. Picking it up, she was convinced it was Sam, calling back to renege on his promise.

"Hello, Marcie," a woman murmured in dulcet tones.

To Marcie's astonishment, her caller was Dacinda—Sam's mother and, for the time being, at least, her mother-in-law. Much as Marcie admired her, she'd always been somewhat in awe of her. The older woman's formidable combination of personal strength, understated wisdom and effortless Southern charm had always made Marcie feel a little brash.

They hadn't talked since Marcie's separation from Sam. To her credit, Dacinda had expressed sorrow over the breakup. But she hadn't blamed anyone.

"Well, Dacinda," she managed. "What a surprise to hear from you...particularly tonight."

"I imagine it is, dear." The words contained an audible chuckle. "In case you were wonderin', I just talked with Sam. He told me about your upcomin' visit. I just wanted you to know...you're stayin' here."

Marcie's eyes widened. "You mean...with *you?* Honestly, Dacinda...I don't think that's such a good idea."

"Nonsense, dear. You're still family as far as I'm concerned. Besides, the Spoleto Festival is in full sway. Hotel rooms will be scarce. I absolutely refuse to take no for an answer."

Although aware that an observation point in the heart of Sam's family would be highly advantageous from a journalistic point of view, Marcie didn't want to use her mother-in-law's generosity that way. "You realize I'm writing a story on Sam," she said. "And that, wherever I stay, I'll have to be objective."

"Don't you think I know that?" Dacinda's laughter was as evocative of well-being as sunlight. "I don't own a newspaper for nothin'," she reminded Marcie. "Your room will be waitin' for you."

"Then..."

"If you write the truth about Sam, I'll be satisfied. And I know that's what you'll do."

Marcie hesitated. She couldn't think of any other objections. "All right, if that's how you feel," she said. "I'll be there on Thursday."

Not a word about our pending divorce, she thought as she put down the phone. Maybe I'm right, and Sam wants to expedite the divorce so he can remarry. If that's what he's up to, she'll want to smooth the way for him.

There *was* another possible explanation. But Marcie didn't put much stock in it. In her opinion, the likelihood that Dacinda was plotting to get them back together wasn't that great. When she and Sam had lived together as a married couple, her mother-in-law had never interfered.

Thursday afternoon seemed to arrive in a rush. Almost before she knew it, Marcie was driving her little red rental coupe from Charleston International Airport to that bastion of Low Country privilege, the East Battery. She had no idea when and where she and Sam would meet. She supposed he'd simply turn up at Dacinda's house—sexy as ever and just as difficult to deal with. Whatever else she did, she couldn't let him see that she still had feelings for him.

Serene and columned, the Jeffords' mansion was just as she remembered it. So was Dacinda. Slim and cultivated in aqua silk with a glowing rope of freshwater pearls knotted about her neck, Marcie's mother-in-law had the air of a society matron well insulated from life's unpleasantries rather than that of a hard-driving newspaper executive. She greeted Marcie with her customary genteel affection.

"It's good to see you, dear," she murmured, lightly touching her cheek to Marcie's. "You'll be sleepin' in the Mimosa Room. Salome's makin' her famous smothered chicken in your honor. You might want to freshen up a bit. I'm havin' a few other guests in to dine."

Sam will likely be among them, Marcie prophesied to herself as she unpacked her things. Who else? His married sisters, Halette Mills and Georgina Herndon, and their husbands were fairly good bets. In her opinion, Halette and Georgina had never really cared for her. From the first, they'd made it clear they'd have preferred Sam to marry within their social set. No doubt they'd disparage any reconciliation efforts on their mother's part.

The Mimosa Room, as Dacinda had called it, was Marcie's favorite. She and Sam had stayed there on a Christmas visit they'd paid to Charleston in 1991. In addition to a canopied rice-design four-poster, it boasted a mahogany dressing table, an overstuffed loveseat upholstered with cabbage roses and a private bath. The wallpaper had a mimosa pattern.

Determined not to be found wanting by Sam or any of the Jeffords females, Marcie showered and slipped into an ivory silk designer dress that served as a subtle foil for her short red curls. In contrast with the shorter dresses she'd worn during the first three years of her marriage to Sam, it had a long, slim skirt that ended just above her ankles. Yet it was anything but prim. It had a deep front slit that offered tantalizing glimpses of her legs.

It was still fairly early when she went back downstairs. Poking her head into the kitchen, she found her mother-in-law sampling Salome's creations and chatting with a blond, freckled girl of about ten she guessed was Georgina's daughter, Lizzie.

"C'mon in," Dacinda invited. "We're just tastin' the fricassee. I think it needs a tad more pepper."

As Salome adjusted the seasoning, Marcie realized she'd been mistaken about the skinny, observant child's identity. Dacinda introduced her as Shelby Reece, the daughter of Jack Reece, one of Sam's former partners in his save-the-turtles effort.

"Wasn't he…" Marcie began and then let her words trail off.

Glancing at Shelby, Dacinda appeared to decide no harm would be done by a simple statement of fact. "Shelby's father was killed last year in a boatin' accident," she confirmed, giving the girl a hug. "It involved a rescue effort during one of our summer storms. Before he forfeited his life, Jack managed to save several women and children. I've been actin' as Shelby's foster mother since then, haven't I, sweetheart?"

Clearly fond of Dacinda, Shelby nodded and returned the hug with interest. Her other parent wasn't mentioned. Something told Marcie she hadn't heard the whole story yet.

Twenty minutes or so later, two of Dacinda's guests—Des Whitney and one of her perennial admirers, silver-haired Britisher Brian Folkes—arrived and joined them in the drawing room for cocktails. Contrary to Marcie's speculation, Halette, Georgina and their spouses hadn't been invited, though Sam was expected.

Serenely, as if she were accustomed to Sam's tardiness and didn't let it bother her, Dacinda led them into the dining room at the appointed hour. As she took her place next to Des with Brian and Shelby opposite, Marcie had to admit the room and the table were exquisitely appointed. It must be a kick to live like this, she thought, admiring the starched white cutwork place mats, heavy old silver and chinoiserie vase filled with hothouse tulips, orchids and lilies that served as a centerpiece.

The table settings were rich but simple—gold-banded Haviland and antique crystal—in keeping with the room's classic proportions. A crystal chandelier sparkled overhead, its reflection glinting from a mirror over the authentic Sheraton sideboard, which held a collection of blue-and-white serving dishes.

They began the meal with Salome's oyster bisque. Though it was creamy and delicious, Marcie wasn't very hungry. Much as she appreciated everyone's efforts to put her at her ease, she couldn't keep her tension from mounting as she waited for Sam to arrive.

With the soup plates removed, they attacked a green salad and feather-light biscuits. Des and Dacinda were talking South Carolina politics when Marcie glanced up at Sam's step in the doorway. Athletic, broad-shouldered, with a wry cast to his features, he looked just the same. Yet, in a way she found difficult to define, he seemed subtly different. He's more relaxed, she decided, more centered than he was in New York. Yet like her, she guessed, he keenly felt the stress of the moment.

She's as beautiful as ever, Sam was thinking, with those bright, boyish curls and that knock-'em-dead figure. Probably twice as smart and talented. It hurts just to look at her. If only we hadn't messed things up the way we did.

Try as he might, a man couldn't rewrite history. Resisting the urge to greet her in some intimate physical way, he wished her a cordial but somewhat reserved hello.

"Hi, Sam. You're looking well," she responded, her voice a little thin.

"Thanks. So are you." Pausing to place a light kiss on his mother's delicate cheek and give Shelby's shoulders an affectionate squeeze, he took a seat opposite hers.

Though she was careful not to stare, Marcie couldn't get enough of looking at him. The old black magic he'd always exerted was still strong enough to constrict her throat and cause her heart to thump to an accelerated rhythm. Simply being in the same room with him was like a drug to her senses. Sam, Sam, she lamented as she lowered her eyes and toyed with her lettuce leaves. What were we thinking, to split up the way we did? Viewed from the perspective of her life without him, their differences seemed so petty.

Emotions are like the skills needed to ride a bicycle...deeply ingrained and far too easy to recall, she thought regretfully as the table talk resumed. Unfortunately, they weren't much use when it came to predicting what would happen between two people. Or plotting the course that events would take. She didn't have the faintest idea if Sam was glad to see her. Or casually indifferent to her presence.

Awash in regret and suffering from a full-blown case of déjà vu, Marcie was quiet throughout the remainder of the meal—downright uncommunicative in Des's Mercedes as they and the other adults who'd gathered at Dacinda's dinner table carpooled it to the Brady Longroom, a ballroom and private club situated on the second floor of a converted theater that had served as a tavern in Colonial days.

Once there, they planned to partake of after-dinner drinks and chat firsthand with a visiting state senator who was expected to run for governor, Des explained. Dacinda wanted him to write a column about the man's aspirations.

As they ascended to the club via a polished oak staircase that skirted the building's first-floor restaurant, Des quietly commented that Marcie was "better looking than ever." But it didn't do much to lift her mood. Only one thing would accomplish that, she guessed: the unequivocal and comforting reassurance Sam had been eating his heart out. She doubted any such encouragement would be forthcoming.

In contrast to the restaurant, with its quasi-modern blend of tapestry-hung brick walls, wrought-iron chandeliers and Victorian sideboards, the Longroom exuded a spare, eighteenth-century ambiance. Set with individual tables for an upcoming private party, the wainscoted ballroom boasted a gleaming, fifty-foot sweep of pine planking.

At one end, the former theater's velvet-curtained stage had been restored to its initial splendor. Directly in front of it, in the area where one might expect an orchestra to set up during theatrical productions, a number of plush chairs and cigarette tables had been arranged. Marcie noted a piano. A stereo. And a portable bar. Several people, including the state senator, had congregated there already. Most had ordered drinks from a white-jacketed bartender.

"Quite a place, isn't it?" Des remarked as they appropriated a velvet-upholstered love seat. "Like most buildings in this part of the city, it has a lengthy history. Charlestonians entertained our first president here when he visited in 1791. No less than fifteen toasts were drunk to the Marquis de Lafayette's health on this very spot during his 1825 tour of the U.S., each accompanied by a fusillade in the street outside."

Though the Longroom's history was interesting, to say the least, Marcie couldn't keep her thoughts from Sam for more than a second. Arriving shortly after they did, he took a seat catercorner to hers. Their knees were almost touching. A basket case, she let the politician's self-serving pronouncements and his listeners' questions go over her head.

Faced with a drive back to the state capital that evening, the balding, gregarious politician took his leave after forty-five minutes or so. Following his departure, conversation lagged a bit. "What do you say we put on some music?" the outgoing young wife of a local businessman suggested.

Her proposal met with immediate favor. In response to a recorded dance tape switched on by the bartender, several couples availed themselves of that part of the polished pine floor that had been left free of tables. Avoiding Marcie's eyes as he nursed a beer, Sam didn't move or comment.

"What do you say, Marcie?" Des asked after a moment. "Shall we give it a whirl?"

Miserable because she'd wanted Sam to ask her instead, Marcie accepted. As it turned out, the *Gazette*'s managing editor was a good dancer, lean and light on his feet. But he wasn't Sam. No amount of imagining could make it so. He returned her to her seat just as Georgina Herndon, the older of Sam's two sisters, her husband, Jim, and a stunning brunette Marcie hadn't previously met joined their group.

Dacinda introduced the brunette as Carolyn Deane. "Carolyn's related to us about as closely as Des is," she explained for Marcie's benefit. "In other words, she's Sam and his sisters' third cousin."

Always quick to scent competition, Marcie didn't have to be told that Carolyn had her hooks set for Sam the moment he was free. It was written all over the woman's pretty face. I'll bet they've been to bed together, Marcie thought with a visceral stab of anguish. I suppose it was too much to expect he wasn't sleeping with someone. No doubt Halette and Georgina were delighted with his choice. Unlike her, Carolyn was a childhood friend and native Charlestonian.

If she guessed at Marcie's unhappy train of thought, Dacinda gave no evidence of it. Accordingly, Marcie was stunned when, at the beginning of the next song, her soft-spoken mother-in-law insisted Sam dance with her.

"Humor me for old times' sake," she exhorted him, her mouth curving at his startled expression. "There's no reason to think you and Marcie aren't friendly, is there, now that you've agreed to give her an interview?"

There wasn't any civilized way Sam could refuse. Setting his half-empty beer bottle aside and getting to his feet, he held out his hand. "It would be my pleasure, Marcie," he said.

Somehow she managed to rise to the occasion, let him lead her onto the abbreviated dance floor. Her cheeks burned with pleasure and embarrassment as he rested his jaw against her temple. Pressing against hers, his body's hard, tender bulk was a powerful aphrodisiac.

As fate would have it, Dacinda had chosen a slow, romantic number—one that brought back heady memories. They'd danced to it at a friend's wedding in New York several years earlier, and returned to their apartment to make steamy, passionate love.

Is Sam thinking about the way we moved that afternoon? Marcie wondered, succumbing to helpless frissons of desire. Does he remember how hot it was, with the air-conditioning on the fritz and just a fan to cool us? We must have lost five pounds apiece, rolling and sweating on that mattress.

Tugging her closer, Sam answered her question. At least, he responded to its essence. Careless of what his mother, Carolyn Deane or the other members of their group might think, he insinuated his lower body against her.

The inevitable stirring of his arousal unleashed a flood of emotion. Dear God, Marcie thought, oblivious to the semicircle of curious faces that must be watching them. I'm still in love with him. And I don't want to be... do I? She was afraid that, all posturing aside, love was exactly what she felt.

She almost stumbled when, without any warning, he put her from him, though he continued to imprison her hands in his.

As he stood there, looking down at her, Sam's eyes contained a question. "Like I told you on the phone," he said, not quite asking it, "this is loggerhead nesting season. I'm due on the turtle patrol in a couple of hours."

Would he simply walk out, then? And leave her trembling? Unsure what he expected, she didn't answer him.

Dammit, Marcie . . . you're not making this any easier, Sam thought. He supposed he'd have to spell it out for her. "You wanted an interview, didn't you?" he growled impatiently, tightening his grip. "Well, now's your chance. Come with me to Edisto tonight."

Chapter Three

In two more hours, she realized, it would be midnight. They'd have to stay over at his Edisto place, an isolated cottage at the edge of a marsh, if Glenn was to be believed. Unless turtle-patrol volunteers made a habit of crashing on his floor or appropriating his living room couch, they'd have it to themselves. It was the kind of get-away lovers dreamed about.

Nothing will happen unless you want it to, she assured herself. Maybe not even then. Just because Sam got all hot and bothered on the dance floor doesn't mean he wants to have sex with you. Or that he'll invite you into his bed. Spending the night under his roof is a matter of convenience, that's all. Endangered sea turtles nest by moonlight. If you want photos of Sam attempting to save their eggs, that's when you'll have to get them. Afterward, you'll both need to get some sleep.

She supposed she'd better pack a toothbrush.

"Suits me," she said, careful not to let the excitement she felt creep too blatantly into her voice. "I'm not exactly dressed for it, though. Okay if we stop by your mother's place first, so I can change my clothes? I also need to get my tape recorder, camera and notebook."

Sam grunted his assent. Belatedly he let go of her hands. "I need to pick up some stuff, too. Are you ready to go? Time's a'wasting."

Bidding their companions good-night felt a little awkward. Though Dacinda seemed pleased by the turn of events she'd helped to orchestrate, Georgina certainly didn't. Neither did Carolyn Deane. As Marcie and Sam headed for the stairs, the two women gazed after them and exchanged disapproving looks.

Parked in a nearby alley, Sam's Jeep gleamed from a trip he'd taken through the car wash for Marcie's benefit. About to get in, he remembered his manners and walked around to the passenger side to open the door for her.

"Just like old times," he murmured as she moved past him to take her seat. A moment later, he wanted to kick himself. What the hell was she going to think if he went around making remarks like that? That he'd spent the past two years missing her?

Marcie gave him a puzzled look as he got behind the wheel. What old times was he talking about? "You didn't have a Jeep when you lived in New York," she reminded him.

"You're right. I didn't," he conceded. "As usual, I was just being facetious."

Sitting side by side like a couple after spending so much time apart felt a little strange, yet incredibly familiar— rather like a waking dream. Bemused, they didn't converse much as they drove the short distance to Dacinda's house. Though it was illegal to do so, Sam parked out front.

"I'm already late getting started for the beach," he told her, removing his keys from the ignition and thrusting them into his pocket. "If you could make it quick, I'd really appreciate it. I'll run in and say good-night to Shelby while you get your stuff together."

Racing up the stairs ahead of him and heading into the Mimosa Room, Marcie stripped off her silk dress and panty hose. The room had no closets, and she hung up the dress in an oversize wardrobe she guessed dated back to Civil War days. Next, substituting a stretch-lace camisole for her bra, she pulled on tan shorts, a light blue Henley T-shirt, which she left partly unbuttoned, and a short-sleeved khaki bush jacket. In place of her high heels she donned hiking shoes and socks. Her bare legs were pasty white, not suntanned, but what the heck? She was a redhead. And a city girl. She was supposed to have a pale complexion.

Aware they probably wouldn't return until the following afternoon, she crammed a change of underwear and an oversize T-shirt for sleeping into her camera bag along with her camera equipment and the notebook she'd mentioned. Let's see ... what else? she prodded herself. Toothpaste, toothbrush, skin cream, deodorant. Might as well throw in some perfume. The tape recorder's in my purse. That's it, I guess. Surely Sam has some sort of shampoo on the premises.

Halfway out the door, she darted back to snatch up a foil packet from her cosmetic bag and conceal it in a zippered pocket inside her purse. Like an idiot, she'd brought protection with her to South Carolina even as she'd tried to convince herself she and Sam wouldn't get involved in anything sexual. You must be out of your mind, she thought. Just because the physical attraction is alive and well ...

She almost jumped when Sam appeared in the room's partly open doorway.

"Ready?" he asked.

She nodded guiltily. What if he'd caught her in the midst of that last-minute maneuver she'd pulled?

Though he was clearly in a rush, Sam paused and gave her an appraising look. "The complete macho female reporter, I see," he commented. "Too bad you left that little bit of lace peeking out of your low-cut neckline. It spoils the effect."

Marcie didn't trust herself to accept his offer to come in and look around when they parked in the courtyard of his historic single house. Though she was curious to see how he lived, and even stood up partway in the Jeep so she could see in through the windows during the short time he spent inside the house, she didn't want to picture herself living there. Fantasizing over a scenario that would never come to pass was just asking for heartache.

Still clad in his dress shirt, maroon tie and gray sharkskin slacks, Sam emerged before she could change her mind, and stashed several items behind the seat. They were quickly on their way. As they headed down to Edisto via U.S. 17 and a series of lesser routes that wound through woods and marshland toward the coast, he invited her to question him.

She'd been expecting something of the sort—telling herself he'd get down to business so they wouldn't have to socialize. She'd tucked the tape recorder into her purse for just that purpose. Taking notes at sixty miles an hour with the moon for illustration wouldn't have been very productive.

Sam had left the Jeep's top down. Her hair ruffling in the breeze though it was too short to blow very much, she pushed her miniature machine's Record and Play buttons, and fired away. "Let's start with the turtles," she suggested, "since hopefully we'll be seeing one tonight. What got you interested in them? How did the patrols get started? Do you fund all the expenses yourself, out of your receipts from 'Male Animal'? Or do you seek outside contributions? Tell me about your volunteers."

Relieved to be on neutral ground, Sam was both comprehensive and expansive, to the extent of providing details she hadn't asked for, but which might prove helpful. By contrast, he couldn't help squirming when she began to quiz him about the egging he'd received at the upstate women's college earlier that month. Wishing he could simply forget the whole thing, he kept his answers brief.

"Why do you think feminists are so offended by your strip?" she persisted.

Any number of quips came to mind, none of them appropriate for publication. "I've asked myself that question a hundred times if I've asked it once," he admitted at last. "And come up with a lot of different conclusions. Maybe feminists dislike 'Male Animal' because some of the points my characters make about them are valid. Or maybe they lack a sense of humor. Could be I'm just their current target."

Far from sure she'd extracted a definitive answer from him, though his careful quote wasn't a total evasion of her question, Marcie fell silent as they neared Edisto Bridge. Having visited the island once before, during an earlier trip to see to Sam's family, she recalled a rickety structure spanning a marsh-bordered inlet. In her memory, the road past it led to a tin-roofed schoolhouse, brooding oaks that made a canopy draped with Spanish moss. To her, Edisto had seemed a magical place, a timeless world set apart composed of gleaming wetlands, shadowy woods and windswept beaches, the whole of it serenaded by an undulating symphony of crashing surf and hidden bird calls.

As they emerged from a patch of trees and the inlet came into view, she saw a new bridge had been erected. It was big and impressive looking, a triumph of modern engineering that would stand up to the most ferocious hurricane, she guessed. Knowing Sam's predilections in such matters, she flung him a sympathetic look.

"Progress," she snorted.

He rolled his eyes. "You got that right, babe . . . if by progress you mean more tourists. Give developers an inch, and they'll gobble you right up."

The narrow road leading toward the beach and the trees that lined it were the same. But the schoolhouse was boarded up. A new one with less character and a dearth of history had probably been built at another site. Keeping her thoughts to herself so as not to sadden the man beside her, she counted a single grocery store, scattered cottages, a motley collection of churches that had been around awhile. The verdict was more hopeful than she'd expected. Progress hadn't won the battle yet.

Though he'd stopped at his house in town to pick up a sack of clean laundry and a portfolio containing the current work on his strip, Sam still need to change. Instead of heading straight for the beach, they turned down a dirt road and pulled up beside a ramshackle cottage. Nailed together of wavy cypress boards and scrap lumber, it had sagging screens, a tin roof and a rusting water tank. It was situated at the edge of a marsh, as Glenn had said.

"I'll just be a minute," Sam said. "You can come in if you want."

This time, Marcie took him up on the offer, hastily turning her back when she realized the "bedroom" where he unabashedly started removing his outer garments was little more than an uncurtained alcove off his combined living, kitchen and work area. The cottage was pure Sam: clutter, a complete lack of pretentiousness, cozy but mismatched furnishings.

As always, his work area was an island of efficiency. The wall above it had become a kind of bulletin board. Densely layered with clippings, sketches, postcards and photos torn from magazines, it drew the eye like a magnet.

Casting her eye about the rest of the interior, she noted a few puzzles and comic books that had been left out on a rickety coffee table. Shelby's? she wondered. From what she'd gathered that evening at the dinner table, the orphaned girl and Georgina's ten-year-old Lizzie occasionally paid him a visit there. Try as she would, she couldn't discern any evidence of a woman's presence.

With scarcely a wasted motion, as if he realized how awkward their unaccustomed familiarity was for her, Sam completed the change to work shirt and shorts. Yet he didn't let her totally off the hook. Methodically massaging bug repellent onto his exposed skin, he offered to perform a similar service for her.

Irrationally convinced he'd guessed how hungry she was for his touch, Marcie turned him down and applied the repellent herself with hasty, haphazard strokes.

Watching her and recalling the fierce, do-it-yourself independence that had sometimes gotten her into trouble, Sam shook his head. She was going to get bitten and that was a fact. Well, he had stuff for bites, too, in his medicine chest.

Getting back in the Jeep, they drove to the nearby home of Sam's chief lieutenant in his save-the-turtle effort, graying commercial crabber and Edisto native Joe Bain. An old friend, Joe knew he and Marcie were separated. White teeth flashed in the man's ebony face as Sam introduced them, identifying Marcie as "my wife, I guess."

Aware of the discomfort his remark had caused her but unable to stop himself from baiting her, Sam went on to explain that she'd come to South Carolina to do a story on him. The story would include their work with the turtles.

"No need to worry over the fact that we have differences," he said. "If there's one thing Marcie understands, it's how to be objective."

The crabber's grin broadened. Obviously he'd decided Sam was teasing her. "Nice to meet you, Miz Jeffords," he said.

"The name's McKenna, Joe," Sam corrected.

Marcie couldn't help wincing. She didn't want him embarrassing Joe to get at her. Or to revisit the tussle over her maiden name that had been one of their major sticking points.

Giving her a surprised look but declining to press for an explanation, Joe tossed a couple of shovels and several large white plastic buckets in the back of the Jeep, and climbed aboard.

To Marcie's relief, Sam got off her case on their way out to the beach, explaining for the benefit of her story that Joe accompanied him on most turtle patrols. The crabber also watched over the eggs they routinely transfered to a wire-mesh enclosure on his property, he told her.

Buried in plastic buckets of sand inside the enclosure, the turtle eggs hatched safely beyond the reach of predators like raccoons, Sam said. Once the baby turtles had emerged from their shells and tunneled their way to the surface with their tiny flippers, he and Joe released them on a darkened beach.

"The darkness of the beach is important," he noted. "Instinct prompts the hatchlings to head for the moon, which trails an inviting beacon of silver over the ocean while it's still in the east. They get confused on a beach where artificial light is present. Sometimes they head the wrong way. Too many get crushed beneath the wheels of campers and speeding hot rods."

They picked up the fourth member of their party, University of South Carolina graduate student Tim Cross, at the weathered hulk of the Edisto Beach canteen, where he'd parked and locked his motorcycle. A moment later, they were on their way, drifts of oyster shells crunching beneath the Jeep's tires.

The air was cool, the breeze pleasant as they passed behind a string of weathered beach cottages Sam remarked were owned "by white folks who drive down from the city on weekends." Few appeared to be inhabited. While Tim raked the sand with a spotlight for evidence that nesting had taken place, Sam drove and tuned in the radio. Linda Ronstadt's rendition of "Blue Bayou" was playing on the station that came in most clearly and he left it on. For some reason, it added the perfect nostalgic note.

Probably none of this would be happening if Sam hadn't stayed out all night following the awards banquet, Marcie thought. We'd still be living together in our Manhattan apartment, still fighting over petty junk. Then again, she supposed, maybe they wouldn't. The way they'd been behaving toward each other, something else would have come along to separate them.

Whatever the case, she could see Sam had found his element. From an almost palpable awkwardness over her presence at the dinner table, he'd relaxed into his familiar routine. He plainly loved the beach and life in South Carolina. Being where he wanted to be and doing something that interested him to save the environment had given his life an enviable resonance.

In one way, its apparent seamlessness left her out in the cold. Yet in another, it comforted her. She loved Sam enough to wish him happiness. *If only I could believe there was room for me in what he's doing now,* she thought, deliberately forgetting for the moment that her job was still tied to New York, not to mention home and all the associations that entailed.

Conversely, though for the most part her thoughts seemed to be expressing themselves in a minor key, she had a profound sense of exhilaration. *It isn't just the moon, the music and Sam's presence beside me, though all those things are part of it,* she told herself. *It's the possibilities.* It was anybody's guess what would happen when they returned to his cottage by the marsh. Just thinking about it made her break out in goose bumps.

When they reached the tip of the island, they turned around and retraced their route, passing behind the beach cottages again and continuing beyond the canteen, into the state park area. A few campers and pup tents were nestled among the scrubby vegetation and scattering of palms that covered a low dune formation. Though no one approached to ask what they were doing, they caught the occasional firefly glow of a cigarette and snippet of conversation.

A little farther on, the dunes leveled off to a man-made hummock of sand that separated beach and marsh. There were no more campers—just tidal pools, the moon, the hiss and boom of the breakers.

At last they reached the wind-silvered gash in the island's anatomy that was Jeremy Inlet. Beyond, the beach stretched wild, untouched. They could go no farther by Jeep, Sam announced. The inlet was too swift and deep for his vehicle to cross. Occasionally he and Joe went over by motorboat, looking for eggs on the sand that stretched beyond it. They almost always rescued a clutch or two. Mostly, though, they cut the critters that liked to dine on turtle eggs some slack. Beyond Jeremy, the baby turtles usually weren't subject to human threats.

As they began their second pass, the wind died down. Marcie found herself swatting incredibly tiny, bloodthirsty insects with increasing regularity. The bug repellent she'd used didn't seem to be working very well. Could it be the tiny creatures were attracted by her perfume?

"What do you call these darn things, anyway?" she asked finally in frustration.

Joe chuckled to himself, a rich, throaty sound. "They be 'no see'ums,' ma'am," he said. "I always heard tell they liked pretty women best."

"Well, they're eating me alive!"

Taking pity on her, Sam extracted a plastic squeeze bottle from his shirt pocket and handed it to her. "Maybe you'd better put on some more gunk," he said.

Though they made five round trips of Edisto Beach, they didn't spot any nesting loggerheads. Marcie was keenly disappointed. "I can't very well write about them if I haven't seen one," she complained. "Besides, Glenn ordered pictures."

Sam paused in the act of checking his watch to give her a level look. "There's always tomorrow night," he suggested.

It was going on 3:00 a.m. by the time they let Tim off at the canteen and proceeded to Joe's place for a beer. Yawning contentedly though she was at the prospect of another evening with Sam, and despite her enjoyment of the men's companionship, Marcie had begun to itch. Each point of contact between her skin and the marauding insects she'd encountered seemed to be swelling into an individual red welt.

Setting his partially consumed beer aside, Sam bent to examine her legs. "We'd better get you home, put something on those bites," he remarked.

Since they'd left the beach, the sky had clouded up. Consisting mostly of dirt roads that connected a few straggling, unlit dwellings, the way back to Sam's cottage was deserted and dark as velvet. Shutting off the Jeep when they reached his yard and walking Marcie inside the house, he ordered her to strip to her underwear.

"Joe gave me a homemade concoction that's supposed to keep the swelling down and stop the itching," he explained in response to her startled expression.

Self-conscious about the way her stretch-lace camisole and matching bikini briefs revealed the shape of her nipples and hinted at the tuft of red curls that nestled between her legs, she did as she was told. A moment later, he'd returned from the bathroom bearing Joe's home remedy in a recycled cold-cream jar. The look in his eyes as he unscrewed the lid told Marcie her less-than-modest underwear hadn't gone unnoticed. She doubted if he'd missed a single detail.

Abruptly she wrinkled up her nose. Greasy and yellowish, with the consistency of partly melted chicken fat, Joe's concoction emitted a peculiar odor. It wasn't terribly unpleasant, though. In fact, on second thought she rather liked it. As Sam pulled up a kitchen chair and began to smooth the preparation over her affected skin, working his way upward from her ankles and giving her inner thighs all the attention they deserved, she suddenly got the giggles. Maybe Joe played a trick on us, she thought. Maybe it's a love potion.

"What's so funny?" Sam asked, resting a negligent hand on her hip. "Am I tickling you?"

As he spoke, the blue of his eyes was near enough to drown in. He still wants me, Marcie thought.

"No," she answered. "It's nothing. Just a private joke."

"You can tell me, Red."

"I'd better not." The dimple he'd always liked so much flashed secretively beside her mouth.

If she teases me, or sends me a come-on with those big brown eyes, I'm sunk, Sam thought, checking her waistband area for bites and then moving on to her neck and upper arms. Just touching her like this again is making me crazy.

Making love never solved anything between you in the past, the sensible man in him argued. If you and Marcie are intimate, and she heads back to New York without you, it's going to be twice as rough. As for the divorce, you haven't even talked about it yet.

Maybe I ought to find out what's going on with that, Sam thought. But not tonight. Or tomorrow, if I can help it. Shelving his desire, though it was anything but forgotten, he finished spreading Joe's preparation on her arms.

Whether accidentally or by design, he'd neglected to smooth any on her left wrist. She shivered slightly as he lifted it to his mouth and tasted its underside with his tongue.

"Same old wrist . . . salty, tart, not a hint of sweetness," he whispered, raising her eyes to hers.

The feats Sam could perform with his tongue were legend, if memory served. As for the blunt, tanned fingers that held her wrist so lightly, many was the time she'd lost any inclination to call the shots beneath their expert ministrations. A single touch from him and my body comes alive, she thought. I want to feel him inside me again. Mount that passionate spiral. How I wish he would tease me and please me . . . take us all the way to paradise.

If he could read her thoughts, Sam didn't say so. Instead he dropped his hands, put Joe's remedy away and shooed her into bed.

"Where do *you* plan to sleep?" she asked, realizing the moment the words were out that he might take them as an invitation. If he does, so much the better, she thought.

Pausing to unbutton his shirt, he didn't seem to put that spin on things. "On the couch, after a bit," he answered, glancing casually in her direction. "I'm a little keyed-up. I think I'll draw awhile first."

Her sense of letdown almost a physical thing, Marcie switched off the bedside lamp and burrowed against the pillows. True to form, he hadn't bothered with fresh sheets before offering her his bed. The pillowcases carried his scent.

As he plopped down in front of his worktable and picked up a pencil, she vowed to stay awake, capture the texture of his life in memory if that was all she was going to get. Thanks to the quantity of fresh air she'd inhaled and the gamut of emotions she'd experienced since arriving in Charleston that afternoon, she was far too sleepy to do anything of the sort. Yet in a sense she got her wish. As she drifted into dreams, she took the image of Sam with her—naked to the waist in a circle of lamplight, doodling at his desk.

Chapter Four

Sunlight was pouring into Sam's sleeping alcove when Marcie awoke. Her inner clock and subliminal awareness of the sun's position in the sky told her it was fairly late—probably around 10:00 a.m. or so. She was sprawled in her usual wake-up position: flat on her stomach, hugging one of the bed pillows. At some point during the night she'd thrown off the top sheet, kicking it down around her ankles. No doubt she'd given Sam an eyeful.

For several seconds, she didn't move as she tried to recall her dream and listened for his movements. Though wisps of it tantalized, the dream quickly faded, leaving her with little more than a vague impression that they'd been in it together. As for Sam, if he was up and around, he wasn't making much of a racket.

Turning over, she saw that the living room couch was empty though a pair of scrunched-up pillows bore mute testimony to the fact that he'd tried to get some Zs atop its sagging springs. The man himself was absent. Waking up a little more, she spotted a red light glowing on his automatic coffeemaker. He made coffee for us, Marcie thought. And drank some, from the look of things. He must be around someplace.

Meanwhile, her bug bites had almost stopped itching, though the red spots they'd made on her legs and arms were still visible. Getting up and padding across the cottage's unvarnished wood floor in her camisole and panties, she found a mug on one of the kitchen shelves and poured herself some of Sam's muddy, restorative brew. Naturally, his small refrigerator didn't contain any cream. For once, she didn't mind. At Sam's cottage by the marsh, with Sam himself somewhere close by, black coffee was fine with her.

It was steamy hot. Sipping it meditatively, she examined the sketches he'd been fooling around with the night before. Though they were fairly rough, she could see that, once again, he was poking fun at feminists. "I tuned in the weirdest radio station last night," the character Jake was telling his barroom friends. "It was called WPMS. All the announcers were women. And . . . get this . . . they were all angry and wired to the hilt!"

Feeling slightly traitorous to her sex, Marcie couldn't help chuckling. The way Sam's mind worked was a stitch, and that was the truth. Maybe he's right about some feminists lacking a sense of humor, she speculated. Maybe that was partly my problem.

If so, time spent without him had effected a cure. Her mouth still turning up slightly at the corners, she wandered over to his narrow, uncurtained closet and buried her face against his shirts. Several, worn and not washed afterward, carried the pillowcases' scent. I used to inhale it on a daily basis, whenever I held him in my arms, she thought.

Despite their troubles, her life with Sam had been her closest approach to happiness. If only she had the courage to tell him so. She bit her lip as a sudden upswelling of tears pricked her eyelids.

At that moment, Sam was sweating and shirtless. Unable to sleep except in fits and starts, thanks to Marcie's proximity and a host of memories that wouldn't quit, he'd gone out running. Though the dirt roads near his cottage were far less stressful to his joints than Charleston's concrete pavement, they gave like beach sand. As a result, his leg muscles had to toil harder. Meanwhile, the day was going to be a warm one. He'd worked up quite a sweat.

Wiping the moisture from his brow with the back of his arm, he turned into his yard with relief and mounted the cottage's front porch, keeping his footsteps as quiet as possible in case Marcie was still sleeping. About to open the screen door, he paused so as not to embarrass her. Incredibly, she was sniffing his clothes. Ah, Redhead, he thought, his heart turning over in his chest. You were always so damn sensual. The things you used to do...

She wouldn't want him to catch her in the act. Ducking out of sight, he retreated a few paces and approached the door again. This time, he was whistling. When he entered, Marcie was seated on the couch, demurely drinking coffee. He was treated to a vision of her long, long legs.

"How are the bites?" he asked, inspecting them.

She smiled. "Actually, a whole lot better. Joe Bain is a pretty good bug doctor."

Had she been crying about something? He could only guess. The last thing I want, he thought, is to make her unhappy. While he couldn't pretend all his motives had been unselfish, Marcie's obvious unhappiness with him had been one of his reasons for agreeing they had to part.

They gazed at each other without speaking for a moment.

"Want some breakfast?" Sam asked.

Naked to the waist, his hair-roughened torso gleaming with sweat, he was a sight for sore eyes. As for what she wanted, she doubted it was on the menu.

"Breakfast sounds terrific," she answered. "Want some help?"

She'd never been particularly good in the kitchen—couldn't even heat water without boiling the pan dry, if Sam remembered right, though she was a whiz at carry-out. He hadn't been that great himself, he supposed. Yet, of the two of them, he was the better chef.

"Thanks, but I can handle it," he said.

More expertly than Marcie would have thought possible, he cooked eggs and grits. The eggs were over easy, the grits cooked to perfection. He served them up at the kitchen table with tomato juice, toast, more coffee and a banana in its skin. There was only one banana. They'd have to split it.

"Think we can keep from squabbling over it?" Sam joked.

It was the kind of remark that, during their life together, might have sparked an argument. Now she found it amusing. She gave him a lazy smile.

"Only if I get the bigger piece."

Shoveling in eggs and grits, then nibbling daintily on her toast, she thought again how revealing her lace camisole and panties must be. Yet she made no move to cover herself. Why don't I pull on shorts and a T-shirt? she wondered. Am I deliberately courting him?

A moment later, she reflected that the term *courting* was a bit old-fashioned. It had unmistakable connotations of offered commitment. Meanwhile, though in the eyes of the law she and Sam were still married, they wouldn't be for long unless one or both of them called a halt to the divorce proceedings they'd set in motion.

To date, neither had broached the topic. It's possible neither of us will do anything to stop it, she thought with unwanted insight—not even if we end up in bed together. We'll be too busy saving face.

How in the hell am I supposed to keep my hands off her, Sam thought, if she insists on running around in that get-up? Doesn't she know her nipples are poking through, making me want to capture them with my mouth?

Back in the days when they'd lived together, one of his favorite things to do had been to latch on to one of her sensitive peaks through the fabric of some wispy bra or blouse. By the time he had it off, and they were skin-to-skin, she'd always been wild with wanting him.

You couldn't excise memories like that unless you signed up for a lobotomy. But then, who'd want to? he thought. What he wanted was to relive them in the present tense.

Following breakfast, she disappeared into the bathroom to wash and brush her teeth. When she emerged, fully dressed in her shorts and the oversize T-shirt she'd planned to use as a nightgown, they did up the dishes together. Wiping out his battered metal sink with a sponge, Sam settled at his drawing table.

"If I know you, you've got a bunch more questions," he remarked. "Why not pull up a chair and ask?"

It was the reason she'd come to South Carolina, after all. Or at least the reason she'd been *sent.* "Good idea," she replied. "I'll get my notebook."

Digging deeper into the philosophy behind his strip and his opinions about its popularity, as well as revisiting the details of how he'd gotten started in the cartoon business, she scribbled page after page of notes. At last she had most of what she needed from him, with the exception of a firsthand look at how he conserved the eggs of a nesting loggerhead turtle. It was almost noon. Setting his drawing equipment aside, he suggested they hop into the Jeep and drive down to the beach for a swim.

Marcie hadn't brought a suit. However, Sam thought she'd be able to remedy that problem at the canteen gift shop. The suit that fit her best, an inexpensive hot pink bikini, clashed violently with her hair. She decided to get it anyway, after Sam greeted her with an appreciative wolf whistle when she emerged from the dressing room. The way he kept looking at her as they spread out their beach towels did nothing to disabuse her of her purchase.

By daylight, the part of Edisto Beach that was encompassed by the state park was a completely different place from the one they'd patrolled just a few hours earlier. Whereas the previous night they'd had its moonswept reaches mostly to themselves, that afternoon, dog owners were romping in the surf with their pets. Children splashed in shallow pools while their parents rummaged in picnic coolers. Their skinny bodies etched in relief against crashing breakers and a cloudless sky, teenage boys on surfboards were showing off for each other's benefit. Lovers necked on blankets as if the beach were their exclusive territory.

I wish Sam would kiss me, Marcie thought, acutely aware of his muscular, suntanned presence beside her as she smoothed sunscreen onto her freckled, bug-bitten calves. Doesn't he find me attractive anymore? Or is he afraid of derailing the divorce for some reason? Though she'd seen no sign of one at the cottage, it struck her that there might be another woman in his life—waiting patiently for his freedom to become official.

Though he appeared relaxed and casual to the point of laziness, Sam was tangled up in some internal questions of

his own. Red...Red...what am I going to do with you? he
was thinking. You're so sexy and available-seeming in that
pink bikini of yours. Yet you act so cool, as if we're nothing more than acquaintances who've been out of touch.
Why'd you come all the way down here to South Carolina,
anyway? Was it really just to do the story because Glenn
ordered you to? Or did you have another agenda in mind?
If so, I wish you'd give me a hint.

Placing the sunscreen bottle to one side, Marcie stretched
out on her back and shut her eyes. Sam followed suit. On
the sand between their beach towels, the tips of their fingers were almost touching. He's not going to say anything,
she thought, her heart aching. He'll let me fly back to New
York without bringing up the divorce and what we're going to do about it. A month from now, our lawyers will
communicate.

She put her angst over the situation on hold as they
cooled off in the surf, diving beneath the breakers and then
bobbing up like corks, to ride them back to shore as if the
ocean were one giant rocking chair. But it didn't stay forgotten long. Each rivulet of saltwater that ran from his
body when he lay back down on his towel was an invitation to contemplate lost pleasures. He was so close. Familiar despite the years they'd spent apart. Yet maddeningly
out of reach.

"Want something cold to drink?" Sam asked as a dusky
youngster toting a foam cooler approached to hawk his
wares.

Marcie nodded without speaking. Though the lemon-
lime soda she chose was satisfyingly icy, it failed to quench
her deeper thirst. I can't believe I was fool enough to lock
Sam out of our apartment, she thought. I could have listened when he said he spent the night at Jack Donovan's.
It's possible he was telling the truth.

In retrospect, she realized a good part of her rage and the lion's share of her feelings of victimization were a throwback to her childhood. She'd never told Sam about her father's lies and infidelities. He couldn't possibly have guessed how painful his actions would be for her.

Despite his faults, she realized, nobody else could hold a candle to Sam. Nobody had ever pleased her half as much.

As he drained his root beer in several long, thirsty gulps, Sam was experiencing similar pangs of regret. He hadn't come up with any solutions to the problems that had beset them in the past, unless you counted a renewed appreciation of her and the willingness to compromise if that's what it took. Yet maybe that would be enough. If he could just keep Marcie on Edisto a few more days, he theorized, patrolling for sea turtles and sleeping between his sheets, there might be hope.

A little finesse might help to move things along. He had steaks in his tiny, old-fashioned freezer. And a bottle of wine he could put in to chill . . .

Abruptly, as he imagined them sharing a romantic evening, that part of his brain that kept track of upcoming events and obligations called up a mental glimpse of the calendar he'd tacked up over his Charleston workspace. In particular, it directed his attention to a note he'd penciled in just two weeks earlier.

Spoleto/Carolyn/8:00 p.m., he'd scrawled.

"Damn," he swore, bending his empty root-beer can in his frustration.

Startled by the expletive, Marcie turned on her side to look at him. "What's the matter?" she asked.

He shook his head. "Nothing I can't fix."

In a moment of weakness, he'd agreed to escort Carolyn Deane to that evening's festival concert. And then forgotten all about it. In part, he supposed, the memory lapse stemmed from his lukewarm appreciation of string quartets. He suspected it had a lot more to do with Carolyn herself. Though he found her pursuit of him flattering, he had no intention of falling into her net. The one misstep he'd taken on their trip to Columbia had been enough.

He'd call her and say something had come up. Offer his apologies. If she got mad and gave him the cold shoulder henceforth, so much the better. She wouldn't ask him out again.

At his suggestion, he and Marcie returned to the cottage soon afterward. Muttering distractedly that he needed to make a phone call, he handed her a towel and a bar of soap.

"You first," he said. "You know where the shower is, don't you? Out back, next to the water tank. Go easy on the water, if you don't mind. I don't have a well on the property, and I'm forced to catch runoff. It hasn't rained around here in a couple of weeks."

Wondering whom he planned to call and still pondering his outburst at the beach, Marcie went outside in her damp bikini. Gravity fed from the overhead tank, Sam's shower was partly enclosed by a wooden baffle. Availing herself of the privacy it afforded, she stripped and rinsed, then shut off the water flow to soap her body.

She found a discarded shampoo bottle containing a half inch or so of shampoo, and she used it to wash her hair. Without cream rinse, I'm going to be pretty curly, she thought as she stood once more beneath the spray. Let's hope Sam thinks I look good in an Afro.

Using the somewhat skimpy towel Sam had handed her, Marcie dried off, then knotted it beneath one armpit. She then padded back into the cottage and disappeared into its primitive bathroom to dress. As she'd walked in, Sam had been holding the receiver to his ear with the frustrated attitude of someone who's listening to a phone ring in an empty house or office.

I wonder what's so important? she thought again. Did he miss a deadline or something?

Returning with damp hair from his own shower as she emerged, Sam was minimally clad in a pair of running shorts. He couldn't very well try Carolyn again with Marcie listening in. Maybe if he could get her to take a nap...

"I hate to admit it," he said with a yawn that belied the inner tension he felt, "but I'm getting too old the burn the candle at both ends. I think I'll lie down for a while."

Without further discussion, he stretched out on his bed. Watching him from the general area of the kitchen with her hands poised on her hips, Marcie wasn't quite sure what was expected of her. Am I supposed to go out on the porch... make myself scarce for a while? she asked herself. Or lie down on the couch? The fact is, I'm a little tired, too.

Sam's mouth softened as he looked at her. She was so pretty and stubborn-looking with that mass of carrot-colored ringlets. Yet so thoroughly ingenuous. When she didn't bother to keep them in check, emotions played over her face like heat lightning.

He hadn't always read them very well.

"I won't bite. You can come lie down beside me if you want," he told her gently.

The invitation was impossible to resist. Incredibly, some thirty seconds later, they were lying side by side on his mattress with their heads on adjoining pillows, the way they had each night when they'd lived together in New York. Well, not quite, Marcie admitted. When things were still good between us, we couldn't seem to get horizontal without making love to each other. It was out of the question now, of course. She'd been an idiot to bring that foil packet with her, as if the past could simply be erased.

It was a turn-on to lie so close to him. Yet she had to admit she was spent. Searching for turtles at 3:00 a.m. had taken its toll. Gradually her breathing became soft and even. Pale and innocent of makeup, her lashes fluttered against her cheeks.

At one point, she thought she heard Sam get up and dial the phone again. Of course, she might have imagined it. He didn't speak to anyone and, by the time he returned to her side, she'd gone back to sleep. Bereft of pride and scruples in her drowsy state, she turned onto her side and nestled against him.

Two hours of heat, limp screens and cicadas later, she stirred and opened her eyes. Sam was still beside her. It seemed he'd been watching her. At once, his expression became guarded.

"That was a pretty good nap you had," he said. "It's nearly 6:00 p.m. I was just about to wake you."

He's acting as if he has an appointment, she thought. I don't get it. We're not due on the turtle patrol until after dark.

"What happens now?" she asked. "Do I ask you some more questions? Or do we send out for a pizza?" She left a little space for him to fill.

Edisto had no pizza delivery service. It scarcely mattered. Sam hadn't been able to reach Carolyn. Food was the last thing on his mind.

"What happens now," he answered, cursing fate, "is that I get dressed and drive into Charleston."

Marcie's eyes widened. "But why? I thought we were going out again tonight."

Sam grimaced. "We are."

"Then . . . I don't understand."

The words fell from his lips reluctantly. "I've got a date for tonight's Spoleto festival."

It was as if he'd flung a bucket of ice water in Marcie's face. To think she'd been mooning over him! "Sorry," she mumbled, getting to her feet and avoiding his eyes as she started to gather up her things. "I should have realized my visit wasn't the only thing on your agenda."

She'd gotten the wrong impression, just as he'd known she would. His voice held a note of desperation. "There's no need for you to leave," he argued, reluctant to get involved in a lengthy explanation of his relationship with Carolyn, because there were aspects of it he'd rather not discuss. "You can stay here," he added. "I'll be back as soon as I can...no later than midnight. We'll go out on patrol the way we planned."

Like hell we will, Marcie thought. Glenn can hire somebody from the *Gazette* if he wants loggerhead pictures!

She was willing to bet his date was Carolyn Deane. Squaring her shoulders, she assumed a casual air. "That's okay," she said. "I need to talk to Dacinda anyway. And interview your sisters. If I don't make it back out here before I have to leave for New York, we can get somebody local to shoot our pictures for us."

She was cutting off all possibility of a reconciliation. Yet he couldn't blame her. I'd have bowed out twice as fast if some guy had shown up and hung all over her, he thought. It occurred to him that maybe there *was* such a guy in her life—one who shared her love of city life and picked up after himself.

I should have let Carolyn twiddle her thumbs, he reproached himself. Even if it would have been a rotten thing to do. This is the rest of our lives we're talking about.

Meanwhile, having decided she'd said too much, Marcie clammed up. If she wasn't careful, Sam would guess how much her heart hurt. She didn't want her pride to take a beating, as well.

Though Sam tried to draw her out once or twice, she was determinedly noncommital on the trip back to town. "Don't be mad at me, Red," he pleaded as he let her out in front of his mother's house. "This date of mine . . . it's no big deal. I didn't even initiate it."

Stung, she pretended not to hear. Since Sam's departure, she hadn't dated.

"I'll call you, okay?" she suggested brightly. "I've got your number. Have a fun evening."

Dapper in a silk suit and tie, Des Whitney was pacing Dacinda's drawing room as Marcie walked in the front door. *"There you are!"* he exclaimed, catching hold of her arm. "I tried to call you at Sam's place on Edisto but nobody answered. Dacinda said he'd be driving back to town this evening and that you'd probably come with him. I know it's last minute. I'd have asked you sooner if I hadn't expected to work late tonight. But a friend of mine had to make an emergency trip to the dentist. He gave me his Spoleto tickets for this evening. Would you possibly consider . . ."

If they hurried, they could make the opening curtain. Along with the chance to attend a first-rate concert, her mother-in-law's managing editor was offering her a glimpse of Sam in action. Plus—she had to admit it—the chance to make him squirm. It was an opportunity not to be missed.

"I'd love to, Des," she answered. "Just give me a couple of minutes to dress."

Thanks to a mad scramble on Marcie's part, they made it to the Dock Street Theater—a pastel, filigree-trimmed conversion of an old Charleston hotel, Des told her—with time to spare. According to him, she looked lovely. Having done her best to outshine Sam's date, whoever she turned out to be, Marcie supposed his characterization was just. Panty hose in a suntan shade camouflaged her rash of bug bites. Hair spray had tamed her unruly curls. The pale blue sundress she'd tossed in her luggage at the last minute was distinctly figure-flattering.

So why were her insides churning like the inside of a blender? Would attending the concert with Des turn out to be a mistake? *I can't let Sam know how difficult it's going to be for me, seeing him with someone else,* she thought. She gave Des a smile to compensate.

The theater's interior, which utilized building materials from old Charleston houses, resembled that of a London playhouse in the early eighteenth century. They spotted Sam and Carolyn at approximately the same moment, as an usher pointed out their seats. "Talk about coincidence," Des whispered as they excused themselves and started down their row.

Marcie didn't trust herself to comment.

The seats Des had inherited were almost directly in front of those occupied by Sam and his date. Mercifully they were a few feet closer to the center of the auditorium.

Your turn to be surprised, Marcie thought, seething inwardly as Des greeted Sam and Carolyn with a friendly hello. *Two can play at this game.* She couldn't help feeling a measure of satisfaction. Carolyn appeared surprised and none too pleased to see her. The expression on Sam's face was downright comical.

Marcie can't have been planning this while we were still out on Edisto, he was thinking. *When I told her about my date, she didn't have one.* It bothered him more than he could say to see her in another man's company.

Carolyn recovered her composure first. "How nice to see you again, Marcie," she drawled, resting a light but possessive hand on the sleeve of Sam's suit jacket.

You don't own him yet, Marcie shot back silently. And you won't, if I have anything to say about it. I'll drag out the divorce till doomsday if you're the rainbow at the end of it!

"I was just thinking the same thing," she responded sweetly. "What do you say we do lunch before I leave for New York?"

Sam wanted to clap a hand over Marcie's mouth at the suggestion. Or, better still, toss her over his shoulder, caveman-style, and head for the Jeep. But he couldn't. For once, he'd act civilized. The moment he got her alone, though, he'd give her a piece of his mind. And apologize. Apologize. *Apologize.* Though it would infuriate Carolyn, he toyed with the notion of asking Des to switch seats.

The house lights flickered, saving him from himself. Without further ado, Marcie and Des took their places. A moment later, the lights had dimmed altogether. Enthusiastic applause greeted the evening's performers as they appeared to take their initial bows.

Mozart's sweetly rational String Quartet no. 19 in C was the first selection. By rights, it should have had a calming effect. Unfortunately, for Marcie, it didn't. Her hands resting in her lap and her gaze ostensibly fixed on the stage, she could feel Sam staring in their direction. I hope you're pleased with yourself, spending an evening with Carolyn when I'm only going to be in town for a few more days, she told him silently. It'll serve you right if you get a stiff neck.

Though it took just a half hour to play, the Mozart quartet seemed interminable. At last its fourth and final movement, the Allegro, came to an end. The musicians' performance had been flawless and they received a lengthy ovation. Once again the lights came up. According to the program, there'd be a brief intermission.

Like many of their fellow concert-goers, Marcie and Des got up to stretch their legs. "I understand wine and soft drinks are available in the lobby," Des remarked. "Shall we partake?"

Marcie nodded. Anything so we don't have to make small talk with Sam and Carolyn, she thought. I don't trust myself not to be a shrew. Or give him cause to think I'm still in love with him.

About to exit via the far end of the row, which had emptied out more completely than the side they'd entered, they didn't count on Sam's desire to smooth things over with Marcie, or his penchant, despite his best efforts to the contrary, for causing her some sort of public embarrassment when they were feuding.

As he reached past a frail-looking elderly couple who'd been seated next to Des, in an effort to tap Marcie on the shoulder, Sam's sleeve caught on the fastener of the birdlike wife's imitation pearl choker. The forward motion of his arm caused the necklace to tighten. She let out an undignified screech.

For a split second, Sam didn't realize he was literally connected with what had taken place. His eyes widened when he realized he was the perpetrator. "Oh my God...ma'am, I'm so sorry!" he exclaimed, thoroughly mortified. "Here...let me help!"

In the commotion that followed, people stared and whispered. The woman's husband hovered ineffectually. As Sam struggled to disengage himself, the necklace broke with an audible clatter. Pearls scattered everywhere, bouncing off the woman's shoulders and rolling under the seats. Apologizing profusely, he did his best to gather them up. In her halfhearted attempt to help, Carolyn skidded on one of them. She plopped awkwardly back into her seat.

"Should we . . . ?" Des asked.

Get involved in *that?* Marcie shook her head. It had been a bad idea to come in the first place. Seeing Sam with Carolyn had given her an upset stomach. Taking Des's arm, she let him lead her to the lobby area.

"What is it with Sam, anyway?" her escort demanded with a shake of his head a few minutes later as they sipped the Chablis they'd promised themselves. "You seem to bring out the worst in him. Remember the awards banquet a couple of years ago? And the whipped cream he was instrumental in getting on that woman's bosom?"

How could I forget? Marcie thought. His behavior that evening was the catalyst that caused our breakup. Heartsick that Sam would choose to interrupt the subtle accord she'd felt growing between them on Edisto in order to take Carolyn to the concert, she shrugged. She barely gave him and his date a second look as she and Des returned to their places.

Chapter Five

The ache of a reunion that had brought Marcie pain instead of pleasure refused to unclench in her stomach as she and Des settled back to listen to the string quartet's remaining selections. I shouldn't have come to Charleston, she thought. Glenn was wrong even to suggest it. I should have put up a better fight.

Now that she was in Charleston and the inevitable had occurred, the best plan would be to complete her interviews with Sam's sisters and Dacinda as quickly as possible, in her opinion. Take an early plane home. And do her best to forget wild, half-buried yearnings. Her facetious suggestion that she and Carolyn "do lunch" notwithstanding, she planned to give the predatory brunette—and Sam—a wide berth for the remainder of her visit.

At last the concert was over. Lingering through several curtain calls, the audience began to file out of the theater. To Marcie's relief, they didn't run into Sam and Carolyn. The bells of St. Philip's Church were tolling the hour as she and Des walked the two-and-one-half blocks that separated them from his luxurious automobile. It was still early. A beautiful night for turtle-seeking by moonlight, she thought. Despondent over the way things had turned out, she wanted nothing more than to return to her mother-in-law's house for the night and burrow into the bedclothes.

"I doubt it'll be an easy sell on my part after the way Sam's performance brought back so many memories," Des acknowledged as he helped her into the Mercedes's passenger seat. "But there's a party getting under way at Buzz Alston's house. Buzz and his wife, Beverly, are the co-chairs of this year's festival. Their home is quite a showplace. You might enjoy seeing it. As managing editor of the local paper, I'm expected to put in an appearance, I'm afraid."

Marcie was certain she'd heard something her first night in town about Carolyn being on the festival committee. No doubt that meant she and Sam would be present, too. Much as it hurt seeing the two of them as a couple, she was seized by a perverse urge to do what Des was suggesting.

She frowned, torn between pride and her single-minded preoccupation with the husband she still loved. "I thought you were planning to work late before the concert tickets materialized," she said. "Don't you have to go back to the office?"

Des shook his head. "I finished up early for a change. So tell me...what's your pleasure? If you refuse, I'll just have to go solo."

If she turned him down, she'd probably regret it. Besides, she *liked* Des. It was just that she'd rather argue with Sam than have a lovely evening with Des.

"Actually, I'd like to go," she said after a moment, "provided we don't have to stay too late. Tomorrow's going to be a fairly busy day for me. I'm hoping to finish the remaining interviews for my piece on Sam . . . see about flying home a couple of days early . . .''

Des's brows lifted slightly. "You just got here. Are you that anxious to leave?"

She couldn't bring herself to lie to him. Accordingly, she laughed and shook her head. Teasing her about New Yorkers being in a perpetual hurry, Des drove the short distance to the Alstons' Civil War-era mansion, which was situated on the South Battery, facing the leafy green of Battery Park and the breezes off the harbor.

Thanks to the number of party-goers who'd preceded them, they had to park several blocks from their destination. The Alston home was lit up like a Christmas tree. Luminaria—candles stuck in sand-filled, brown paper bags with cutout designs—festooned the sidewalks and front steps. As they approached the threshold, Marcie spotted Sam's Jeep. It was parked a block away in the opposite direction. Here goes nothing, she thought, the sick feeling she'd experienced earlier reasserting itself in the pit of her stomach. If Carolyn's draped all over him, I'll find it pretty hard to take.

A butler with white gloves and a patrician expression opened the door for them. Decorated in authentic antebellum style with richly gleaming Sheraton furniture and numerous ancestral portraits, the Alstons' elegantly proportioned, high-ceilinged rooms were awash with people. Tuxedo-clad waiters circulated with trays of drinks. Talk and laughter, the ceremonial clinking of glasses, swirled about them in little eddies.

The largest crowd had migrated to what Des called the formal drawing room. Its reflection puddled on polished wood flooring and duplicated by a quartet of gilt-framed mirrors, a massive crystal chandelier blazed with real wax candles. Painted a pale blush color, the wainscoting glowed apricot. A trio of local musicians was sequestered in one corner. They were partially drowned out by the party chatter as they played a series of classical selections.

"Care for some wine?" Des asked as a waiter approached.

She'd drunk a glass earlier that evening, during the concert's intermission, and she wasn't one to imbibe much alcohol. Still, she needed some sort of boost. "Thanks, I believe I would," she said.

Selecting a glass of Chablis for her, Des didn't take one for himself. "If you'll excuse me for a moment, I need to find a rest room," he told her. "Back in a sec."

A half smile frozen on her face in the event Sam or Carolyn happened to be watching her, Marcie sipped at her wine and tried to look as if she were enjoying herself. Dacinda and Sam's sisters are involved in every charitable and civic event that takes place in this town, she reasoned, retreating into professional considerations. They're bound to be around here someplace. It would make sense to locate them, try to set up some interviews.

Glimpsing Marcie through a break in the crowd, Sam ditched Carolyn at a buffet table in the next room and started in her direction. Unaware of his approach, Marcie jumped, nearly spilling her wine, when his hand closed possessively on her arm.

"Red..." he importuned, determined not to leave things as they stood, though he wasn't sure by any means exactly where he was headed.

To Marcie's relief, he didn't have Carolyn in tow. "I see you made it out of the theater in one piece," she taunted before she could stop herself. "Tell me...did that poor woman manage to collect her pearls? I hope her throat wasn't injured when the two of you got hooked up together."

Sam looked as if he'd like to turn her over his knee. Or affix a permanent gag to her mouth. Fortunately, he'd never been the type to resort to violence. Ignoring her slurs, he didn't dignify them with an answer. Instead he came straight to the point.

"I'm going back to Edisto tonight. If you want . . ."

She didn't let him finish. "Don't you have a date to dispose of first?"

Already Des was making his way back toward them from across the room. A few more seconds and Carolyn would probably catch up with him, Sam supposed. He and Marcie would get busy trying to convince their respective dates that they were indifferent to each other.

"That won't take long," he vowed. "Are you coming with me? If you need those photos . . ."

Marcie really did want the turtle shots. And a lot more besides. She just wasn't willing to ask for it. The situation's hopeless, she told herself. He's dating other women. And I'll be going home to New York in a few days. Accepting his offer will just prolong the inevitable.

"I suppose I ought to," she heard herself relenting, as if she'd planned to do so from the first.

He didn't give her an opportunity to renege. "I'll pick you up in three quarters of an hour at my mother's house," he informed her. "Or better still, at Carolyn's apartment complex on the Ashley. It's called Rivertree, and it's on Des's way home. He knows where it is."

Marcie was frowning again as Des joined them. "Why must we meet there?" she protested.

Already planning his excuses to Carolyn, Sam was uncommonly brusque. "Because it's on our way and I don't want to lose any more time than I have to," he said. "Forty-five minutes. Don't be late."

For the remainder of their brief sojourn at the Alstons' party, Marcie ignored Sam—as he did her. Yet she'd distinctly warmed to him. He'd reopened a door she'd all but convinced herself was permanently shut. Though she had no idea where the gesture might lead, the prospect of finding out was irresistible.

Des didn't argue with her need to work on her story or her request for a lift to Carolyn's place when she explained it to him. He was philosophical when she thanked him for his forbearance. "No thanks are necessary," he said. "As a fellow journalist, I understand the demands of the profession all too well. I just hope we'll be able to spend some additional time together before you leave. There's something I want to talk to you about."

"I hope so, too," Marcie replied. Her thoughts on Sam, she didn't stop to ask herself what Des had in mind.

They returned to Dacinda's house long enough for Marcie to change and repack her overnight bag, then drove to Carolyn's complex. Sam's Jeep was already there, parked outside the building he'd specified. He and Carolyn were nowhere in sight. Are they saying fond good-nights in her apartment? Marcie wondered with distaste. Or quarreling about how the evening went? Either way, she wasn't about to walk up to the door and ring the bell. Stifling a groan of uncertainty, she started to get out of the Mercedes. She'd sit in the Jeep until Sam emerged.

Des wouldn't hear of it. He'd be glad to wait with her. At last Sam appeared, frowning and straightening his tie. Apparently Carolyn had mussed it.

"Time to go," Marcie said in a small voice, picking up her overnight bag.

To her suprise, the newspaper editor leaned over and brushed her mouth with a kiss. "Call me when you get back to town, okay?" he requested.

Suddenly aware how dense she'd been not to realize Des had designs on her that went beyond friendship, she nodded. "I will," she promised. "Thanks for everything, Des. Good night."

Sam's jaw was set as she transferred to the Jeep. Turning his key in the ignition and revving up its engine, he headed out of the complex without a word. His silence lasted a good five minutes. Then, "Did you have to let him kiss you?" he asked irritably. "You're still a married woman, you know."

Marcie's hopes returned in a flood. "Isn't that lipstick I see on your chin?" she shot back, energized. "What about the way your tie was out of whack?"

His scowl deepening, he didn't answer her. They were still at odds when they arrived at Joe's place, bypassing Sam's cottage altogether. Entering as if he owned the crabber's modest abode, Sam used its curtained-off sleeping area to change into a khaki shirt and shorts.

"You guys ready?" he barked when he emerged, as if they'd kept him waiting.

Joe gave him an appraising look. "I been ready for a coupla hours," he noted. "You the one who's been out partyin'."

Pausing just long enough to apply bug repellent, they drove to the beach and picked up Tim at the canteen as they had the night before. It was a few minutes after midnight.

"I hope to hell we didn't miss any turtles, fooling around in town the way we did," Sam remarked testily as they lurched onto the sand and headed south, creating tire tracks behind the beach houses.

Seated beside him in the front seat, Marcie gave him a level look. You were the one with the date, she told him silently. *I* certainly didn't initiate tonight's escapade. Even as she framed the silent comeback, the knot of unhappiness his rendezvous with Carolyn had caused to form in her gut relaxed a little. He didn't want to go, she thought with a burst of affection and indulgence. I'll bet she conned him into it.

The night air caressed his skin as the waves rolled hypnotically to shore with a rhythm that matched his heartbeat, and Sam felt the tension draining out of him. Unless he was very much mistaken, Marcie had just suppressed a smile. Apparently she'd forgiven him for his tryst with Carolyn. And started enjoying herself.

As he kept his eyes peeled for evidence of turtle crawls, it struck him that she still had feelings for him. Exactly what kind of feelings, he had no idea—any more than he knew precisely what he felt for her. A moment later, he admitted he was kidding himself. The truth was, he knew perfectly well. He was nuts about her. In two years, he hadn't met her equal, let alone anyone who could come close.

Still, their situation was complicated. His body wanted her. So did his heart. Each time he admitted them, his head responded to their needs by urging caution. In every way except sex and love, a satisfying man-woman relationship, he'd made a life that fit him like a second skin. Unfortunately, it wasn't the kind Marcie had ever wanted.

If you have half a grain of sense, he admonished himself, you'll take things slow. You and Marcie hurt each other big-time a couple of years ago. Neither of you wants to endure that kind of emotional torture again.

Mentally allowing his mixed emotions to simmer on the back burner, he switched on the radio and concentrated on the task at hand. To his disappointment, as they continued to patrol, no dark shape lumbered out of the surf. Or strained to lay eggs above a laboriously dug pit. He'd promised Marcie a turtle. Yet he couldn't even spot a trace of the characteristic pattern in the sand that signified one had been there earlier.

Following three complete passes of the beach from its southern tip to Jeremy Inlet, they continued to come up empty. It was going on 2:30 a.m. when Tim abandoned his searchlight momentarily to retrieve a can of soda from Joe Bain's ice chest. Accordingly, it was Joe who spied the laboring sea creature first.

"There be yo' turtle, Miz Jeffords," he announced triumphantly, reverting to the use of Sam's surname as he pointed oceanward with one gnarled finger.

Instantly Tim switched off the light. Sam cut the engine as Marcie grabbed her camera. They piled out, edging closer, taking their cues from him. As if by tacit agreement, nobody uttered a syllable.

She was just emerging from the breakers: two-hundred pounds or so of instinct-driven, prehistoric, endangered beast. Barnacles, seaweed and phosphorescent plankton clung to her shell. Beautifully designed to speed her through the watery deep, her flippers struggled awkwardly with the unfamiliar medium of the beach, gouging a series of little depressions in the sand on either side of her body as she lurched clumsily toward her chosen nesting site, above the high-tide mark as her genetic programming had taught her.

"This might take a while," Sam whispered in Marcie's ear, lightly draping an arm about her shoulders. "I'd appreciate it if you'd wait to take your photos until she's actually laying eggs, so we don't frighten her back into the ocean. Once she starts, she'll finish the job. You can use your flash . . . even touch her then, if you want."

Marcie nodded silently as they continued to monitor the turtle's progress. As she watched, she was filled with awe, an all-encompassing sense of wonder that caused the skin on her bare arms to prickle. As for the man beside her, suddenly, inexplicably, she felt close to him. She sensed his relief when eventually the turtle halted, not in a clump of the wiry marsh grass he'd told her could cause problems for nestlings but in unobstructed sand, and rested for a moment.

With an air of predestined, mute compliance to nature's demands that was somehow poignant, the turtle settled into position and began to dig, scooping out sand in crumbling globs and spraying it behind her with her broad hind flippers. As she labored, the salt glands near her eyes began to weep, making her appear to cry bitter tears, as if the process of giving birth was painful.

"Where's her mate while all this is going on?" Marcie asked, keeping her voice low.

Sam's breath was a light touch against her neck. "Waiting just offshore," he answered. "Males don't emerge on dry land. They spend their entire lives in the ocean."

At last the hole in the sand was about ten inches wide and twenty inches deep, according to Marcie's calculation. Again the turtle rested, as if to gather strength.

"Here they come," Joe said, switching on a flashlight and shining it in the vicinity of the turtle's tail.

They moved closer, close enough to observe the process's most minute details. One after another, the turtle's eggs—nearly one-hundred soft, white "Ping-Pong balls" dripping a clear, gelatinous substance—plopped in the hole. Elated, Marcie switched on her camera's motor drive and glanced at Sam for permission.

"Fire away," he said, taking pleasure in her excitement. "Nothing you do now will disturb her."

Swinging into her professional mode with the ease of drawing breath, Marcie began framing her shots with lightning quickness. Her camera's motor drive whirring, she got close-ups of the eggs dropping into the hole and the turtle's teary, ancient-looking eyes, medium shots of Sam on one knee beside the laboring beast, group shots of him with his assistants. The breakers crashed in counterpoint, broken only by the men's low conversation and the deep sighs of the turtle's breath.

At last her egg production slowed, then ceased altogether. Once again, her flippers went into action as she flung sand back into the hole. In a final act of protection for the clutch of eggs she wouldn't return to again, she heaved herself off the nest and sprayed sand backward with her paddle-shaped front flippers to camouflage it from predators.

Checking her shell for metal tags and measuring it with calipers, Sam made several notations in a pocket-size notebook. His hand rested on the small of Marcie's back as they watched the turtle lumber back toward the ocean.

"Get what you wanted?" he asked.

She nodded. "You know I did." Words won't be adequate to describe it, she thought.

She took a few more pictures as Sam, Tim and Joe dug open the nest with care and transferred its precious contents to sand-filled plastic buckets. The night's work was almost finished. It was time to deliver the eggs to the wire-mesh enclosure Joe had built for them, return to Sam's cottage and hit the sack.

Given the lateness of the hour—it was almost 4:00 a.m.—they didn't stay at Joe's long. They were sweaty, sandy and exhausted as they drove into Sam's yard.

"I can't wait to get under the shower," Marcie commented, reaching under the Jeep's front seat for her overnight bag.

"Neither can I," Sam agreed.

As he'd watched Marcie capture the nesting loggerhead on film and taken pleasure in her delighted competence,

Sam had overcome his better judgment. If he didn't seize it, he'd convinced himself, the opportunity her visit to South Carolina afforded him might slip forever from his grasp.

"Maybe we ought to shower together," he added. "My water supply's running pretty low."

A twinge of desire shot through her at the outrageous suggestion. "I don't think…" she began as they started for the porch.

Having dared to say what was on his mind, Sam refused to backtrack. "You don't have anything I haven't seen, and vice versa," he reminded. "Neither of us has to look."

It was the kind of reasoning that made sense only at that hour and in that kind of place, one far removed from the conventions of everyday existence. Letting herself flirt with the notion, Marcie didn't answer as he fetched each of them a towel. Her steps lagged only a little as she followed him back outside, to the enclosure beneath his water tank.

Appearing to take her assent for granted, Sam dropped his shorts. She averted her eyes, but not before she'd glimpsed the hard planes of his back and buttocks.

"Coming?" he asked, keeping his back to her as he stepped beneath the shower head and pulled the chain.

"I…guess so." Drawn by the water's mineral-laden rush and the seductive thought of sharing it with him, she was buffeted by waves of longing. Stripping quickly so as not to change her mind, she got in behind him.

Tepid to cool, smelling of rain and the tank's tin lining, the water felt wonderful. So did the proximity of Sam's nakedness. With a sigh of pleasure, she reached around him for a bar of soap.

Though she didn't consciously intend it, her breast brushed his arm. Aroused, Sam turned to face her. Her lips parted, her hair clinging to her head like wet silk, she met his eyes without flinching. Seconds later, they were in each other's arms.

It was the old allure, magnified a thousand times by too many lonely nights, the bitterness of regret that had gnawed at them both. Yes, oh yes, Marcie thought, half out of her head with wanting him as the hard column of his desire pressed against her thighs. I need to be part of you again. Feel you inside me so deeply that we're like one person. Any second now, he'd hoist her up and she'd wrap her legs around him, exult in his upward thrust of entry.

Afterward...

The thought of what morning might bring inserted a sliver of doubt in her happiness. If she let him love her, would he say goodbye as if it had never happened? Let the divorce go through without raising any objection? Imagining the effect such an outcome would have on her, she drew back a little. "Sam...I'm not sure we ought to do this," she objected.

Heated past the boiling point, Sam decided not to force the issue. He didn't want to give Marcie anything to regret, fresh cause to be angry with him. *If only I knew how to bridge the gap that separates us,* he thought.

"Whatever you say, babe," he answered, crushing her mouth with a lingering kiss before letting go of her and shutting off the water.

A moment later, he was wrapping her in a ragged, skimpy towel. Overcome by the nurturing gesture, she felt tears sting her eyelids. "Sam," she whispered. "I didn't mean..."

"Hush." He kissed her again, this time as if she were a contentious two-year-old. "It's okay," he added gently. "We can talk about it later, if you want."

He was still naked and, almost as an afterthought, he knotted his own towel about his hips before following her into the house.

Avoiding each other's eyes, they dried off and dressed, Marcie in a clean T-shirt and bikini panties, Sam in undershorts. It was time to sleep, and a single question consumed them both. Fierce with the need to reestablish their aborted closeness, Sam decided to answer it. Stretching out on his bed, he plumped the pillow next to his.

His invitation was clear. Marcie hesitated less than a heartbeat before taking him up on it.

Reaching up to turn out the overhead lamp as her weight settled against his bedsprings, Sam plunged them into darkness. Gradually their eyes adjusted. The soft rhythm of their breathing flowed together as they lay side by side—close but not quite touching.

I can't bear it if he doesn't hold me, Marcie thought.

So quickly it seemed that Sam could read her mind, she got her wish. "Come here, Red," he bade her gruffly, drawing her into the curve of his arm and offering the comfort of his shoulder.

Chapter Six

An hour later, the first squally raindrops of a long-overdue shower began to fall, hitting the tin roof of Sam's cottage and running into his elevated water tank. A breeze rushed up, riffling his sagging window screens. Its cool breath caused Marcie to stir. Half-drugged with sleep, she became aware that something—the hair on Sam's chest?—was tickling her nose. Awakening a little more, she caught a whiff of his essence, the faint but unmistakable skin scent that was uniquely his. She'd have known it anywhere, even on a crowded street. In some elemental way, she thought, giving her imagination free rein as she drifted in her hyper-awareness of him, we're still husband and wife, mismatched puzzle pieces that, by some miracle, fit together.

In the middle distance, thunder rolled. Abruptly, it started to rain harder, clattering on the roof, the tank, a pair of rusting metal chairs Sam had placed outside the window with a view of the marsh in mind. Churned up by the downpour and permeated with the salt tang of the ocean, the aroma of moss-hung woods and the bitter green smell of marsh grass stole into their presence.

With a mutter of protest, Sam woke up, too. And realized he was happy. Incredibly, *Marcie* lay beside him, nestled in the place his heart had stubbornly maintained for her during the long nights of their separation. Reaching down as he had so many times in the past, he pulled up the top sheet and covered them. His right shoulder prickled from lack of circulation but he didn't mind. It felt better than he could say just to hold her.

He'd forgotten Carolyn, along with the mess he'd made of his and Marcie's fragile affinity the day before. His ear keenly attuned to the rise and fall of Marcie's breath, the rhythm of her heartbeat, he decided she was awake, too.

"You'll never know how much I want you, Red," he whispered.

Caution gave way in her at the admission, collapsing like a sand castle in encroaching surf. So did her scruples. "Oh, Sam . . . I want you, too," she blurted, her words muffled against the pulse at the base of his throat.

With a silent benediction that was part longing, part dumb animal relief that he'd get another chance with her, he drew her fully into his arms. Mouth to mouth, their legs tangled up together, they set about reclaiming what they'd so sorely missed.

I want to feel her skin-to-skin, Sam thought. Her T-shirt was in the way. He planted a kiss on her bare midriff as he helped her out of it. Uncovered to his hands, her breasts were small but perfectly shaped, their nipples taut with arousal. He knew from experience how sensitive they were—capable of telegraphing stimulation to her deepest places in the blink of an eyelash, she'd told him.

"I can't wait to taste you," he said, drawing one of them into his mouth. Thumbing the other with light, suggestive strokes, he had her crying out with pleasure in seconds.

For Marcie, it was as if a key had been fitted to the lock of her separateness. A creature of instinct like the turtle she'd photographed, she enfolded him, mutely begging him to take her.

Too often as he'd lain there in his sleeping alcove, staring out the window, Sam had dreamed of caressing the warm, silken length of her from her calves to her exquisite shoulders. I want to knead her buttocks, he thought, deliberately fueling his desire. Gather her close against me. Still wearing her bikini panties, she wriggled to help as he dragged them from her hips.

"Now you," she demanded breathlessly.

Disposing of his shorts, he tossed them on the floor. He and Marcie rolled onto their sides, facing each other. Freed of restraint, his male attributes jutted against her. A sigh escaping her, she took him in her hand. How beautifully made he was, how wonderfully shaped. The skin that sheathed his distended flesh was soft as a baby's as she stroked him to readiness. To touch him that way after such a long, lonely time was unbelievably erotic. One thrust of him inside me and I'm liable to lose it, she thought.

Transported by her caresses, Sam had no intention of letting their first experience in two years begin and end that way. Pushing down an almost overwhelming urge to enter her, he slipped a finger into her velvet folds. Though it had been a long time since they'd made love, he found the focus of her need in seconds.

With him, Marcie had always been quick, profound and helpless. Relaxing against the pillows and speading her knees apart, she took immense pleasure in abandoning herself to his will. Somehow he'd known what she liked, from the very first, and given it to her without stinting.

Gradually the crescendo of her fulfillment built, acquiring a rhythm of its own. As she neared her apex, she tilted her body upward, gathering purchase with her feet. For one elongated moment, she trembled at the brink, knowing the outcome was inevitable. Seconds later, heated chills swept over her skin as she let the tremors take her.

At last she quieted, the slight nasal congestion coitus always gave her making its presence felt. "Sam..." she began in the tone she'd always used when she was about to demand something.

"Don't talk, babe." He kissed her cheek. "You'll spoil the effect."

"But you didn't..."

"I will. We aren't going anyplace."

As they lay with his arm about her and his lips lightly brushing her forehead, she thought how gentle he could be, how completely unselfish. How much she loved him still! I never stopped, she admitted. Not even when I was angriest at him. She wondered if she had the courage to tell him how she felt.

She could show him, at least, without betraying her vulnerability. Bring him to the peak of pleasure he'd reintroduced to her. She lightly raked her fingers through his mat of dark chest hair, and traveled lower. A moment later she duplicated their loving progress with her mouth.

His little sighs, the defenseless way he meshed the fingers of one hand in her cropped red curls as if to assert possession and, simultaneously, steady himself, confirmed that her catalog of what turned him on was up-to-date. He likes this, she thought, stroking him. And this. Most especially *this*. Bestowing a series of blunt little kisses, she took him in her mouth.

Sam was half out of his head at the sensations she was evoking. His universe contracting to the microcosm they shared, he lost himself in the sweet excess of the moment.

He wasn't the only one succumbing to that state. Just as they'd always been, the pleasures Marcie brought him were their own reward. As renewed arousal pierced her to the quick, her caresses grew more passionate. She wanted Sam again. Deep inside her. Carrying her with him to what she knew of paradise.

Unresolved questions about whether their marriage would continue were the farthest thing from her mind as she raised herself and straddled him. They'd always communicated effectively without words when they were having sex and, a moment later, they rolled over by mutual consent.

Lovingly he entered her. I'm home, he thought. Deep in the Redhead. His face a mask of ecstasy, he began to move, riding high against her and connecting their points of provocation with each downward stroke.

How long they labored there, oblivious to wildly creaking bedsprings and the plops and drips that were all that remained of their rain shower, Marcie couldn't have said afterward. No more than a few minutes, perhaps. They were both ripe for the kind of apotheosis that would shake them to their foundations.

They didn't miss a simultaneous send-off by much. Sam went first, as Marcie had hoped he would, uttering a series of wordless cries that were primitive in their intensity. She followed in seconds, shuddering beneath his weight as their mingled sweat dampened the bedclothes.

Gradually they quieted, each thinking their private thoughts. "You're one hell of a lover, Red...did you know that?" Sam asked, his voice drowsy and warm as cocoa.

The corners of her mouth lifted slightly. "You always used to say so."

"Well, I was right. About that, at least."

His oblique reference to the problems that had separated them twanged a minor string. We can't avoid the past, she thought. Eventually, we'll have to deal with it. Maybe if we start by focusing on the good times, what was *right* about us...

Resurrecting an old habit, she played casually with his chest hair, which she'd always adored. "Remember that Sunday we went to Enid Haupt Conservatory and Amerigo's with Karen DiLiso, my old boss at *Outdoor Magazine?*" she asked.

Sam wasn't quite sure. If he remembered correctly, Marcie had quit *Outdoor* to go to work for *Zoom* shortly before their first anniversary. The name Karen DiLiso didn't mean anything to him.

"You know," Marcie prompted. "She was the skinny blonde with horn-rimmed glasses who had so much greenery in her office, you needed a machete to get near her desk. She kept giving me plants and you kept killing them ... accidentally, of course, though I'm not sure she believed it."

He grinned. "Oh, yeah. I do remember her."

"The week before we went to Enid Haupt, there was a staff party at Mort Zelnick's apartment. That morning, your cartoon about the man who grew plants instead of chest hair in an attempt to please his environmentally conscious wife came out in the paper. Karen didn't think it was funny. She organized that trip to the Bronx to acquaint you with the error of your ways and indoctrinate you in her way of thinking."

Sam's grin broadened. The incident Marcie was talking about was coming back to him. "She lectured me every step of the way through the Victorian Palm Court and the Fern Forest," he recalled.

"Yes, she did. You nodded like the meekest of husbands and didn't say a word of protest when, all the time, you were gunning for her."

He planted a fond kiss on the tip of Marcie's nose. "As a matter of fact, I was."

"I don't know how you stood it until we got to Amerigo's. Karen was still on her kick, holding forth about plant sensitivity and the need to create as much green space as possible in the world as we looked over the menus. It wasn't until we ordered . . ."

"And the waiter asked me what kind of salad I wanted . . ."

"That you unbuttoned your shirt. And said in your best stentorian voice, 'I don't need one. I brought my own.'"

Sam chuckled. "Gluing those fake plants to my chest was no easy matter. I spent so much time in the bathroom that morning, you threatened to call the fire department."

Though she'd been mortified at the time, Marcie was laughing, too. "Karen was really shocked, wasn't she?"

"So were you."

"I'll never forget the way her face looked, if I live to be a hundred. I thought it would crack and fall off in her service plate."

"Now there's an idea . . ."

His cartoonist's mind was always casting about for the offbeat humor in things. It was one of his most endearing qualities. So was his concern for the environment, one that translated into action, dwarfing her former boss's puny commitment. She'd just begun to realize how many such traits he possessed.

Unexpectedly she grew wistful. "We had a lot of fun in those days, didn't we, Sam?" she asked. "I miss them so much...just as I've missed you."

"Dammit, Red..."

Turning onto his side, he took her back in his arms. "Thinking about what we threw away two years ago isn't going to get us anyplace," he emphasized. "This is now. And we're here in bed together. In case you're worried I've somehow lost it, I still have my proclivity for publicly embarrassing you."

Though it hadn't seemed terribly funny at the time, Marcie couldn't help smiling at her mental picture of Carolyn Deane skidding on the elderly woman's pearls and collapsing into her seat like a three-legged giraffe. The humiliation she'd suffered had served her right for chasing Sam, when he still belonged to Marcie.

"I'm sorry for being so mean at the theater tonight," she said with a shake of her head. "We should have stopped to help. When Des asked if I wanted to, I said no."

Holding and stroking her had given Sam another erection. "No apologies," he told her firmly. "We need to get some sleep. Before we do, though, maybe we ought to have another nightcap...."

He wasn't talking about alcohol. No dummy, Marcie didn't need a slide rule to figure it out. Warmly in favor of another round of lovemaking despite the tiredness that had begun to creep into her bones, she sought his mouth with parted lips.

Rosy after the night's dark pall, the first, barely perceptible paintbox tints of another day were streaking the sky over the marsh by the time Marcie and Sam fell asleep. They were dead to the world when, shortly after 9:00 a.m., Dacinda's cherry-red Volvo turned into the yard and parked beside Sam's Jeep. Chattering like magpies, Shelby and Lizzie piled out before Sam's sleek, sixtyish mother could turn off the ignition.

"Shh!" she cautioned, holding one perfectly manicured finger to her lips. "Have you forgotten Sam is up half the night on the turtle patrol? He might still be asleep."

Shelby considered. "Can we go inside and get out the worm farm stuff we're working on if we're extra quiet?" she asked.

The orphaned girl's reference to their latest science project caused Dacinda to wrinkle her nose. "I suppose so," she conceded, regarding the cottage with a thoughtful expression. "Now remember what I said. *Tiptoe.*"

Fortunately for Sam and Marcie, who'd slept naked as jaybirds with the top sheet crumpled about their waists, the ten-year-olds couldn't stop talking for more than a few seconds. Even when told to hush, their young, high voices carried effortlessly.

Bolting out of sleep, Sam shook Marcie by the shoulders. "Quick!" he exclaimed, locating his undershorts and pulling them on at top speed. "Get dressed! Today's Saturday. Dacinda's brought the girls out from Charleston to sleep over and go on the turtle patrol with us!"

Blinking the slumber from her eyes, Marcie pulled her T-shirt over her head and looked around for her lace bikini bottom. To her consternation, she couldn't find it anyplace.

Sam was on the verge of panic. "I'll look," he offered, making sure his fly was shut and frantically smoothing the bed. "Get in the bathroom, will you, if you can't find your stuff? They'll be at the door in a second."

Snatching up her overnight bag—which, fortunately, she'd left standing in plain sight—Marcie didn't shut herself into Sam's cramped, primitive bathroom a moment too soon. As she dug out a clean pair of panties and put them on beneath cropped light blue denim shorts, she could hear Shelby and Lizzie cornering Sam with questions.

"How about brewin' a pot of coffee?" Dacinda's perfectly modulated voice said.

When Marcie emerged, Sam was busy with the coffee-pot. The girls had spread the components of their proposed worm farm out on his rickety coffee table for assembly. As usual, Dacinda was being herself—calm, collected and stylish. Not a hair was out of place.

The older woman was looking distinctly pleased about something. "Hello, dear," she greeted Marcie from Sam's sole excuse for an easy chair. "I saw you and Des last night, at the concert. Too bad we didn't have an opportunity to chat. By the way, thanks for leavin' that note. I'd have worried about you otherwise."

Despite Sam's attempts to tidy it, his bed still looked rumpled and slept-in. The couch didn't. Aware Dacinda wouldn't have any trouble adding two and two, Marcie wasn't sure how to answer her.

"It was the least I could do," she answered, joining Sam in the kitchen area and quietly setting about making scrambled eggs, bacon and toast.

Declaring herself thoroughly pampered after the five of them had demolished every morsel of the surprisingly successful breakfast Marcie had put together, Dacinda announced she was heading back to Charleston for some shopping and a quick look at the final layout for the Sunday paper.

"So…" Sam addressed his young charges after she'd left. "What do you girls want to do today?"

"Go to the beach," Lizzie proposed at once.

"Visit Joe's and see if any of the baby turtles are hatching yet," Shelby chimed in.

They had time to do both. A budding scientist, according to Sam, Shelby was first out of the Jeep when they arrived at the crabber's place. She ran directly to him when he appeared, limping slightly with arthritis, on his front porch.

"Joe . . . Joe . . . have any of the baby turtles broken out of their nests?" she exclaimed, catching hold of his hands.

White teeth flashed in the ebony of Joe's face as he attempted to settle her down with a mixture of fondness and grandfatherly patience. "Not yet, Miss Shelby. But some be workin' on it. I think they restin', waitin' for the sand to cool. Could be we might see them after dark."

Shelby's enthusiasm only escalated at the news. Nothing would do but to go around back, to the wire-mesh enclosure, immediately. As she and Lizzie raced ahead, the adults followed at a more decorous pace.

"What did you mean about the hatchlings resting and waiting for the sand to cool?" Marcie asked their host.

In his folksy, unscientific way, Joe explained that the turtles' genetic programming called for them to emerge at night when the bright horizon of the ocean would attract them. At that time of day, there were also fewer predators. Somehow they knew that, when the sand was a few degrees cooler, it was dark—and safer—to emerge.

Watching Marcie mentally file away the information, Sam realized how genuinely interested she was in his work. She'd long since jotted down all the notes she needed for her story. And she was still asking questions.

Already feeling exceptionally close to her as a result of their lovemaking in the predawn hours, he gave himself permission to draw even closer. Despite her exhilaration when they'd spotted the nesting loggerhead and her total absorption in photographing it, he hadn't previously thought of his commitment to helping save the species as something they could share. What if she ends up liking it here and can be prevailed upon to stay? he fantasized. Hopes he hadn't dared to admit he entertained took on a more conscious shape.

When Joe finished answering Marcie's question, Sam added a few postscripts of his own. In fact, the hatchlings rested for a brief period below the surface for another reason, too. When they entered the ocean, they would swim frantically for many hours, slackening their pace only when they'd gone a considerable distance. Again the incentive was evading predators, which tended to be more numerous at shallower depths.

At the wire enclosure Joe had built, Shelby and Lizzie were closely scanning the staked and numbered nests for any sign of activity. Including them in his remarks, Sam went on to describe the turtle "elevator" that brings the hatchlings to the surface. As a result of their struggle to emerge from the nest, which usually takes four days or so, he said, the ceiling of the nest caves in. Sand filters down, raising the floor of the cavity where their eggs had been buried, thus lifting them up.

Lizzie was charmed by the elevator concept. "Too bad they can't press a button and come right up to the surface," she said. "Their kind of elevator sounds like work."

Shelby, meanwhile, continued peering through the wire. "Is the little low spot on Number Three a ceiling that's about to cave in?" she asked.

Joe nodded. "That be the one I was talkin' about."

Sam studied the nest in question. Unlike the others, it had a slightly sunken appearance, as if it were a miniature sinkhole in the making. "I agree," he said. "If we're lucky, we may be releasing some baby turtles on the beach tonight."

At the news, Shelby and Lizzie could barely contain themselves. "We have to name them!" Lizzie exclaimed. Chanting provisional names for the tiny creatures, she and Shelby literally danced in a circle. Releasing baby turtles into the ocean would be a first for both of them.

From Joe's, they went to the beach. This time, in addition to the towels Marcie remembered from the previous day's trip, Sam had brought a blanket. They stretched out on it as their charges made a beeline for the surf.

"Don't go too far," he shouted after them. "Those breakers can knock you off your feet."

Shelby yelled back something cooperative but unintelligible that he translated to mean "Okay." He turned to Marcie. "Need any help with that suntan lotion, Red?" he asked, resting an affectionate hand on her thigh.

As Shelby and Lizzie played in the surf and then emerged to build a miniature sand fort for the plastic cowboys and Indians Shelby had brought along in her beach bag, Marcie and Sam soaked up rays and touched each other with circumspect affection. Having slept just a few hours the night before, they also dozed a little. But their charges didn't allow them to get much rest. Ultimately, as a result of considerable nagging, particularly by Shelby, they allowed themselves to be drawn into the water.

It had been ages since Marcie had spent much time around children of any age. They're delightful, she thought. So energetic and intelligent. And Sam's so good with them. Watching the three of them interact, she had to admit he was definitely "dad" material.

Still, she couldn't help wishing that they'd chosen a different weekend for their visit. Because of their presence, any chance for renewed lovemaking had been put on the

back burner. So had the talk she'd hoped would materialize about what was happening between them. With Shelby
and Sam's niece in the cottage, she knew, he or she would
end up sleeping on the couch.

By the time they'd returned to Sam's place and spar-
ingly rinsed the salt from their bodies, Marcie had a slight
sunburn despite the precautions she'd taken. She supposed
it went with the territory of being a natural redhead.

Taking advantage of the opportunity for further touching, Sam smeared gel on the affected areas. "Time for a
nap," he announced, giving her a speaking look.

Though the girls groaned in unison, he stood pat. "No
nap, no turtle patrol," he said unequivocally. "That's the
deal."

Submitting with a minimum of fuss, they pulled worn
sleeping bags from behind the couch and flopped down
atop them on the floor. Reluctantly appropriating the bed
because he knew they'd question any other arrangement,
he threw Marcie a pillow. Her back to the youngsters, she
stuck out her tongue at him as she caught it.

To her surprise, she slept. When she awoke, Sam and his
young visitors were foraging in the refrigerator for snacks
and getting up a card game. "Come play with us, Marcie," Shelby entreated.

Though she'd never been particularly fond of cards,
Marcie thoroughly enjoyed their game of Push, an intri-
cate form of rummy. She particularly liked watching Shelby
in action. To her amusement, the orphaned girl turned out
to be something of a card shark. Her pale, almost nonex-
istent brows furrowed in a frown of concentration
throughout much of the game, she beat Lizzie and her two
adult competitors hands down.

"You're really good. Did you know that?" Marcie complimented her a few minutes later as she got a couple of pizzas out of Sam's freezer preparatory to popping them in the oven. "Where'd you learn to play like that?"

Briefly, a shadow crossed the girl's face. "From my dad," she acknowledged after a moment.

"Shelby, I'm sorry..." Setting the pizzas aside on the counter, Marcie gave her a hug.

"It's okay." Shelby allowed herself to be embraced for a moment, then wriggled free. "Dad was a charter boat captain and fishing guide," she added with seeming indifference. "I used to play with him and his friends when the weather was too bad to be out on the water."

The awkwardness passed, though not without Marcie gaining some insight into the girl's character. She's independent, a little too grown-up for her age because she's had to be, she guessed as they munched their pizza and watched a little television on Sam's tiny black-and-white set. Yet it's easy to see she has a loving heart. She's particularly stuck on Sam. And he clearly dotes on her.

She wondered where Shelby's mother was. Dead? Behind bars somewhere? Or just too selfish to be bothered with her? Thank God for Dacinda.... At least Shelby has a roof over her head and someone caring to look after her, Marcie thought, resolved to ask Sam a few questions about the girl's situation when she got the chance.

The relaxed, sociable atmosphere in Sam's cottage as they hung out, waiting for night to fall, put other thoughts in Marcie's head, as well. This is how it would be if Sam and I had children together, she realized. It might cramp our style somewhat. Yet I suspect that, ultimately, it would bring us closer together. She wanted to kick herself when she recalled the single-minded pursuit of her career that had caused her to postpone giving Sam the baby he wanted.

At last it was time to go. Applying bug repellent and piling into the Jeep, they headed back to Joe's place. The crabber was out behind his house, inside the wire-mesh enclosure. A special yard light he'd rigged up was blazing. On hands and knees by the nest they'd inspected that afternoon, he appeared to be collecting objects and placing them in one of the white plastic buckets they used to transfer eggs from the beach. Within the sandy pen, a number of small, dark shapes had evaded his grasp and scattered in all directions.

"Joe...Joe...did the baby turtles break through?" Shelby squealed.

The old man's throaty chuckle gave him away even before he answered her. "That you, Miss Shelby?" he asked. "Get your butt over here, please, and help me catch these devils!"

Because of the danger of crushing the tiny creatures if too many people got into the pen at once, just Shelby and Lizzie crawled inside to help with the turtle roundup. Though Marcie already had enough photographs, she'd brought her camera and now she fired away, expertly catching the slapstick comedy and uncomplicated delight that permeated their efforts.

Finally all the turtles they could find were secure in plastic buckets with air holes drilled in their lids. "How many do you think there are?" Shelby asked as they loaded them up in the Jeep and started for the beach.

Sam shrugged. "About a hundred, give or take a few," he replied, reaching behind him to ruffle her hair.

Time enough to tell Shelby when she's a little older that most of them will fall victim to natural predators or shrimpers with illegal nets before they reach their first birthday, he thought. Still, if just a handful get through, and the females among them make it back to this beach to nest, we'll have done our work.

It wasn't until they arrived at the canteen—where, for once, Tim wasn't scheduled to meet them—that he remembered something he'd been about to ask Marcie. "I hope you'll send me copies of some of those pictures," he murmured as he drove off the pavement onto the sand and turned north into the state-park area.

How could he have known that his request, so innocently put, would cause uncertainty to flower in her heart and spark a flood of questions?

Chapter Seven

"Of course I'll see to it that you get a set of prints," Marcie said.

Absorbed in choosing a site to release the turtles that was close to their original nest, Sam hadn't been a husband for nothing. During the years he and Marcie had shared a bed, he'd learned to heed subtleties, faint tremors of the lower lip. Though admittedly he was out of practice, something about her tone grabbed at his attention.

"Anything wrong?" he asked, frowning as he glanced at her.

For Marcie, the key word in his request had been *send*. Her reconciliation fantasy evaporating like dew in the warm South Carolina sunshine, she'd pictured herself in her New York office, sliding the photos into an envelope and mailing them to his Charleston address. Back in their separate lives, they'd let the divorce go through by default. Little by little, they'd lose track of each other. The fact that he'd asked for the photos at all led her thoughts in the same direction. It didn't take a Ph.D. to figure out that a duplicate set of photos would be unnecessary if they planned to live together again. They could share an album.

Face it, she thought, mocking herself for her foolishness. Sam has. To him, last night didn't count for anything more than it appeared to be on the surface—a commemorative roll in the hay by two people with a strong sexual appetite for each other and totally incompatible lifestyles. Meanwhile she'd been piecing a future together.

Determined not to bleed in front of him, she put on a happy face. "How could anything be wrong?" she objected lightly, answering his question with a question. "It's such a beautiful night. And we're about to release a bunch of baby turtles. That's something I didn't expect."

Though he wasn't totally convinced, Sam decided to take her at her word. Nodding to let her know he understood, he parked the Jeep on hard-packed sand at the far end of the park's accessible stretch. By now, the moon had risen sufficiently to hammer a path of silver across the ocean's surface. A stiff breeze off the water kept insects at bay. The weather was perfect for their purposes.

Removing the buckets containing the turtles from the Jeep, he set them side by side on the beach a short distance from the surf. Joe pried open the lids. By the moon's radiance, they surveyed the squirming mass of marine life they'd surrender to the elements.

"They have an awfully hard job ahead of them, don't they?" Shelby observed sympathetically.

Sam responded with a shrug. "It's their job to swim out and be part of the ocean's ecosystem," he told her. "Just like it's yours to go to school. Mine to draw cartoons that make people laugh. Joe's to catch crabs, and Marcie's to write stories. So...what do you say? Are you guys ready for the big event?"

Shelby and Lizzie glanced at each other as if they wanted to prolong their custody of the turtles for a few more minutes, then nodded yes. Following Sam's example, they removed the tiny creatures a few at a time and placed them carefully on the sand. At first the babies seemed confused by their freedom and simply milled about, bumping into each other. Several made false starts in the wrong direction.

"Not to worry," Sam said, setting one of the mistaken voyagers straight. "They'll get their bearings in a moment."

His prediction quickly proved accurate. Before long, a veritable tide of scurrying, dark shapes blended with the ocean's far greater one. Lifted by the breakers as they started to ebb, the turtles were quickly afloat. They began to paddle furiously, as instinct directed. As she watched, there was a lump in Marcie's throat.

"Can't we keep just one?" Lizzie begged when finally they were down to a few stragglers.

"Sorry, kiddo. But it's not allowed. Joe and I have a special license to dig up the eggs and protect them. And it says all the hatchlings have to be returned to the ocean. That's because the species is in trouble. To keep from dying out, it needs all the new babies it can get."

Clearly skeptical, Lizzie considered his explanation for a moment.

"Besides," Joe added, "them turtles get *big*. I don't think your mama, Miss Georgina, will want one hangin' around her livin' room."

Saved by the giggles, Lizzie climbed willingly back into the Jeep, while Shelby took up a position next to Joe so she could help him with the light. Marcie resumed her place beside Sam. The night's turtle patrol still lay ahead of them.

As they proceeded down the length of the beach and back again, Marcie did her best to commit the night to memory, savor every moment. Yet the sense of loss she felt was crushing. At least Sam and I are friends again, she thought disconsolately, visually tracing the strong lines of his profile when she thought he wasn't looking. Our divorce will be an amicable one.

No nesting turtles emerged from the surf to distract her from her ruminations. Nor did they spot the distinctive signature of a turtle crawl. Only a beached but salvageable baby shark, roughly two feet long, caught Shelby's eye as she kept lookout.

Setting the Jeep's emergency brake, Sam got out and carefully returned the stranded creature to the water. As she watched, Marcie thought again how good he was with Shelby and his niece, how dedicated to helping save the environment. Now that it was too late, she was seeing facets of him that seemed totally foreign to the smart-mouthed creator of "Male Animal," the discontented misfit who'd chafed at life in New York.

By returning to South Carolina, Sam had come into his own. Despite an occasional scrape, such as catching his sleeve on the elderly woman's necklace at the concert, he was a man in a million—caring, independent, deeply resonant. If only I could believe that what happened between us early this morning wasn't an episode out of context, she thought. That we could make things right somehow.

Unfortunately her job was still tied to New York. And it wasn't difficult to see he was where he belonged. Even if geography didn't stand in the way, she realized, he might not want her back on a permanent basis. His request for the photographs had seemed to indicate as much. Was it possible they'd just backslid into the kind of habit that was hard to break?

Completing their final pass down the beach somewhat earlier than they had the night before because of the girls' presence, they dropped Joe off at his house and continued on to Sam's place. The ten-year-olds didn't protest when Sam ordered them to wash their faces, brush their teeth and hit the sleeping bags. For some time, their tails had been dragging.

Sam and I will sleep as we did this afternoon, Marcie thought, awaiting her turn in the bathroom. And it's probably for the best. Still, she knew she'd make love to him and gladly if she had the chance, whatever his motivation. After interviewing Dacinda and Sam's sisters, she wouldn't have an excuse to remain in Charleston, let alone on Edisto. Accordingly, it might be their last night together.

Though he couldn't guess at what she was thinking, it had occurred to Sam, as well, that she might need to leave for Charleston in the morning. Though he might like to think so, she wasn't on a pleasure trip. She had commitments, responsibilities.

"Come out on the porch with me…split a beer while the girls go to sleep," he invited her when at last Shelby and Lizzie had bedded down and shut their eyes.

Desperate for time alone with him though it would likely be bittersweet, she accepted. It was only when they were safely out of the girls' earshot that Sam revealed his true purpose.

"Ever make love in a canoe?" he asked, his eyes lit with mischief as he laced his arms about her waist.

Her lips parted slightly as the old familiar drumbeat escalated in her blood. Slowly she shook her head.

"I did once," he confessed. "Or tried to, when I was seventeen. It wasn't much of a success. Maybe with the pillows from this old swing we'll have better luck."

He wanted what she wanted. At least for now. At least the physical part. Would it be enough? Maybe, she thought, hope stubbornly reasserting itself, I misread his comment about the photos. Asking me to send him some is natural enough, given the fact that we haven't talked things over yet. Meanwhile, she was aching to hold him.

"Say something," Sam prodded lovingly. "I can almost hear the wheels turning inside your head. If a canoe doesn't turn you on, we can come up with an alternative."

He could be so practical sometimes. And so funny—all in the same breath. A smile tugged at the corners of her mouth. "I'm willing to give it a try if you are," she said.

"That's my girl." Dropping a kiss on the tip of her nose and scooping up the cushions in question, he held the screen door open for her.

As they passed through the cottage's rear yard, Marcie snatched up a beach towel one of the girls had left hanging on the back of a lawn chair.

Sam's ancient canoe was tied up at a sagging dock by the edge of the marsh. It faced what appeared to be the opening of a narrow, twisted channel. The canoe had come with the property when he'd acquired it more than a year earlier, he whispered. He'd been thinking of buying a new one. But he hadn't gotten around to it yet.

As they stepped onto the dock, keeping their movements as quiet as possible, a night bird called, its cry plaintive and unbearably sweet. The air was cool, the sky partly cloudy. Appearing from time to time, like a galleon riding the troughs and crests of waves, the moon lapped gooseflesh on the brackish water and edged the marsh grass with silver.

A broad, grassy expanse typical of the area, the marsh was situated between the solid ground where Sam's cottage and a number of other small dwellings stood and the curving finger of beach where they'd released the baby turtles a short time earlier. To Marcie, the channel, if that's what it was, looked extremely shallow. What if there were snakes? Or alligators?

Seating himself in the canoe's stern, Sam signaled her to pass him the cushions.

"Won't we get lost?" she whispered, handing them to him one by one. "Or run aground? That water looks awfully shallow."

He shook his head. "Trust me, Red. I know what I'm doing."

They didn't exchange any further remarks as she got in, balancing with his help, and took a seat. With just a few strokes of his paddle, they were hidden from view. The only sounds that met their ears were the mating calls of frogs, the muffled splashes of the paddle and the drone of insects.

At last they'd gone far enough from the cottage and the other dwellings that ringed the marsh that their antics wouldn't scandalize anyone. Putting the paddle away, Sam helped Marcie arrange the pillows. They'd have to be careful undressing, he warned, so as not to overbalance his battered craft. A moment later he was pulling his T-shirt over his head and unzipping his shorts, making love to her first with his eyes.

Lit by the desire she saw in them, Marcie followed suit. How beautiful he is, she thought, with that compact build and his thick, dark hair, and with the strains of lust and humor that ran so deeply in him. Oh, I do love him so. It was nothing short of miraculous to her that, after so much time apart, they were lovers again. If she lived to be a hundred, she'd never be able to thank Glenn Bokaw enough for dispatching her to South Carolina over her objections.

Getting situated to indulge their pleasure wasn't the easiest thing of tasks. For one, the canoe's available space was cramped, its metal bench seats arranged at awkward intervals. For another, they were still moving—ever so slightly, it was true, but moving nevertheless. Sam hadn't bothered to run out an anchor and the breeze abetted the marsh's sluggish current. Eventually, if they indulged themselves long enough, Marcie supposed, they'd come out in the ocean, perhaps by way of Jeremy Inlet.

The feelings of despair that had plagued her earlier expunged from her thoughts, she didn't mind the discomfort or inconvenience. Thanks to the cushions they'd brought, the feat they aspired to wouldn't be impossible. Sitting in the canoe bottom on one of them with another propped between her back and one of the seats, she spread her knees and held out her arms.

With a disbelieving little shake of his head, Sam came into them. Is this really Marcie here with me, instead of miles away in New York? he asked himself as he took possession of her mouth. Can this really be happening?

Because of the precariousness of their position, they couldn't move very much. Instead of rolling like thunder, they'd have to take things slow, delight in subtlety. Burrowing lower to taste the velvety texture of her skin, which was as soft as the ocean-scented breeze that fondled their nakedness, he kissed every square inch of her he could reach.

Condemned to lie relatively motionless beneath his caresses though she was able to stroke his back and buttocks, Marcie dissolved in a fever of wanting. The faint movement of the canoe only exacerbated it. So did her sense of immersion in a vast terrain, the great, wild river system that drained the southeast coast.

I want to lose all control, she thought. To be a leaf swept away on the current of his need. I want to be immersed in him. Together they'd explore the tides of the universe. "Sam . . . come into me," she whispered.

How could he deny her, when what she pleaded for was what he wanted most? It would have been impossible for him even to attempt it. Fitting himself against her, he gloried in her readiness. A moment later, he was plunging deep.

The sensation of fullness his entry gave her almost pushed her past the brink. Battling for control, she gripped Sam with her strong interior muscles. No stranger to what she was experiencing, he held himself in check. Only a throb he couldn't control betrayed his corresponding struggle.

Ultimately it was safe to begin their ascent. At Sam's suggestion, which he telegraphed to Marcie without words, they continued to keep their activity at a minimum, concentrating instead on exquisite correspondences, the most subtle of movements.

Marcie found the canoe's barely perceptible forward drift, its blind nudging against clumps of marsh grass as it threaded the narrow, convoluted channel without his guidance, a kind of aphrodisiac. In the stillness between each thrust that united them, a hot, diffuse glow spread through her body. Longing crested in waves, becoming more intense each time Sam withdrew and then restated his claim.

The constraints of maintaining balance evoked his resourcefulness, as well. Feeling his way in a new, incredibly erotic wilderness, he began to find the exquisite rhythms of their carefully orchestrated communion more soul-stirring than the most impassioned rush toward gratification. At the same time, he realized he couldn't last. Already the upward spiral of his need was building, escaping his control as it lifted him to ever greater pinnacles of delight.

With an abruptness that shook them to their foundations, the concentric circles of their arousal deepened. Though they might wish to, it wasn't possible to retreat. Daring to pump himself into Marcie with a mounting fervor that caused the canoe to rock wildly, its sides dipping dangerously close to the water, Sam broke free first. Gooseflesh passed over his skin as he shuddered in his fulfillment.

His rapture and her own willingness to capsize, if need be, ignited Marcie's. She followed in seconds, her tremors implosive and deep. Yes...yes...*yes!* she exulted, unaware the litany of affirmation had escaped her lips.

Their muffled cries of abandonment fading, they clung together in the rush of afterglow. Gradually their sweat cooled. Their breath resumed its natural rhythm. The almost mystical connection that had bound them relaxing a little, they shifted position for greater comfort. With a little sigh of contentment that reached all the way to his toes, Sam drew Marcie's head onto his shoulder. The canoe continued to drift through the marsh like a skiff in an ancient ballad, transporting the hero and heroine to a place of safety, where they could dwell together.

A half hour later, they emerged in Jeremy Inlet as Marcie had predicted they would. Though they were still minus their clothes, Sam had continued to wear his watch. By its luminous dial they read the hour. It was 4:04 a.m.

Time to head back, Marcie thought. We'll be at the beach in a few minutes if we don't. I can almost hear the breakers. Tentatively reaching for her shirt, she paused when Sam stayed her hand.

"We have time for another round on the beach if you're willing," he told her, the smoldering quality of his renewed desire for her too blatant to miss.

Hers rose instantly to meet it. She wasn't sure they should indulge themselves. "Won't there be people about?" she asked.

He shook his head. "Probably not at this hour. Certainly not on the north end, across the channel . . . the part you can't get to without a boat."

A fresh wave of concupiscence washed over her at the prospect of what they'd do together. On the beach their movements wouldn't be restricted. They could ride each other like cossacks, buck with the fervor of wild horses exiting a rodeo chute.

"Let's go, then," she agreed, her nipples tightening in anticipation.

Dipping his paddle into the inlet's deeper, more swiftly running current, Sam had them at the beach in just a few minutes. He insisted Marcie remain seated until the canoe was safely on solid ground. Going over the side in waist-deep water, he dragged it up on the sand and spread out the faded beach towel she'd brought as if it were a potentate's carpet.

"Welcome to my kingdom by the sea, most delectable of redheads," he said with exaggerated gallantry, holding out his hand to her.

So beautifully proportioned, so unselfconscious in that natural setting, Sam set her pulse to racing. As for her, she'd never alighted naked on a beach before, never drunk in the heady ionization of ocean breakers with nothing but her satin skin between her and the elements.

To do so now, to experience it with him, imparted a dizzying sense of risk, a brazen inventiveness that fired her imagination. Empowered by more spontaneity than she'd ever hoped to possess, and with the rhythmic pounding of the surf for an accompaniment, she tugged him down on the beach towel and made love to him with an ardor that left him gasping.

Dawn was streaking the sky when, thoroughly sated and ready for sleep, they tied up the canoe at Sam's dock and sneaked back into the cottage on silent feet. As they'd hoped, Shelby and Lizzie were still dead to the world, sprawled atop their sleeping bags like a pair of overgrown puppies. Kissing each other a lingering good-night that spoke mutely of the profound pleasures they'd shared and their reluctance to be parted physically, even for a few hours, Sam and Marcie took up their separate places on bed and couch.

Tonight's lovemaking was one of our best ... maybe the best we've ever had, Marcie acknowledged as she shut her eyes and reveled in the blissfully relaxed state of her body. Yet it's almost time for me to go. We've said nothing about the future...barely mentioned the past except to recall a few humorous episodes.

For all she knew, she'd still be sending the photos Sam had requested to his Charleston address and wondering why he didn't call. Yet as she drifted into dreams, her thoughts dissolving into disjointed images of an ancient skiff with a legendary, dark-haired captain at the helm, she couldn't seem to help herself. Her mouth relaxed in smile of pure contentment.

Chapter Eight

From Marcie's perspective, full-fledged morning with its raucous accompaniments of bird song and energetic children, came much too soon. So deeply asleep that it was like being at the bottom of a well, she surfaced reluctantly at Shelby's prodding.

A pair of hazel eyes with tiny flecks of gold suspended in their irises were staring directly into hers from beneath pale blond lashes when she opened them. "Is it okay if we make pancakes?" Shelby demanded when it became clear Marcie was actually listening to her. "We're starved. And there isn't any cereal."

Her head a leaden object that seemed permanently sunk in her scrunched-up, misshapen pillow, Marcie tried to focus. Was unsupervised pancake making a safe undertaking for ten-year-olds? Or would they burn themselves? Fill the cottage with billows of acrid smoke?

"I asked Sam, but all he does is mumble and go back to

sleep," Shelby added, her usual breezy demeanor verging on complaint.

A professional dog-walker instead of a baby-sitter to earn spending money during her teenage years, Marcie didn't have much experience with children and their capabilities. Even if Sam had the requisite ingredients on hand, which she doubted, it wasn't likely his kitchen accoutrements ran to electric griddles. Afraid of what might happen if she turned Shelby loose on his balky old propane stove, she scraped herself off the couch.

"Maybe I'd better help," she decided, yawning so broadly, she thought her face would crack. "Just give me a minute in the bathroom first."

Miraculously, Sam's cupboards and small refrigerator contained syrup and the makings of the pancakes Shelby and Lizzie craved. There was even some bacon. With her face washed and her hair brushed, Marcie felt almost human. She decided to make a pot of coffee, too. If memory served, the only thing that penetrated Sam's morning fog after a late night out was the fragrance of freshly brewed coffee. He was her partner in crime—the instigator of their canoe trip to the beach. If she had to be awake at that hour, acting as *chef de cuisine* and kitchen warden for a pair of ten-year-olds, it was only fair that he get up and watch.

Thank heaven she'd committed the cooking school's all-purpose pancake recipe to memory. "Okay, girls," she said brightly. "Let's get started. Lizzie, get down a bowl and break two eggs in it. You know how to do that without getting the shell in them, right? Here...let me show you. Shelby, I need you to find a skillet and some shortening while I try to light this burner...."

Though they'd never shared a kitchen before and Sam's wasn't the most modern or convenient, by any means, Marcie and her youthful apprentices worked together more smoothly than she'd had any right to expect. Her determination to let them do as much of the work as possible found a ready audience. Once or twice, she caught Shelby regarding her with an approving yet somehow thoughtful expression.

His nostrils teased by the aroma of coffee and crisp bacon strips, Sam woke up in time to join them at the table. In an effort to be charitable, he didn't glance at his watch. "What's all this?" he asked, ruffling Shelby's hair as he dropped into his seat.

Marcie smiled. "It's called breakfast."

Fortunately, she'd made enough. Though Lizzie and Shelby were attacking their portions with gusto, there were plenty of pancakes left for him.

As usual, he sipped black coffee first while he completed the waking-up process. Despite the fact that she'd covered the platter with a skillet lid, the pancakes and bacon had cooled slightly by the time he transferred a helping of each to his plate. Hoping he wouldn't be too disappointed, Marcie was gratified by the pleased expression that came over his face when he took a bite.

"Where'd you learn to cook like that?" he asked.

Her smile broadened. "The girls did most of the work."

Sam's gaze traveled from one expectant young face to another. "I don't think I've had better," he said at last, pronouncing his verdict.

The youngsters glowed at the praise. However, Shelby refused to hog the credit. "We used Marcie's recipe," she told Sam earnestly. "I used to burn the ones I made for my dad because I let them cook too long on the first side. Marcie taught us that you have to turn them as soon as the bubbles pop."

The laugh lines that framed Sam's mouth deepened slightly. He raised his coffee cup to Marcie in tribute. "My original question still stands," he said.

She gave Shelby's shoulders a squeeze. "Actually, I took lessons at a Manhattan cooking school. I decided you were right...every fully functioning adult ought to know how to prepare a decent meal."

Flattered that she'd paid attention to one of his complaints and done something about it, Sam shook his head. "Manhattan, huh?" he teased. "I have to hand it to you, Red. These ain't no snooty New York pancakes...no raspberry vinaigrette!"

In exchange for promised time at the beach, the girls did up the dishes and set the kitchen to rights. The buzz of Sam's electric razor emanated from the bathroom as Marcie rounded up her things and packed them in her overnight bag. I don't want to leave, she thought, seized by an attack of melancholy. Much as I enjoy my job and city life in general, I could stay here forever...cooking breakfast on Sam's temperamental stove, sleeping with him at night, accompanying him on the turtle patrol. Making love to him, most especially.

She was romanticizing how things would be, of course. Besides, Sam hadn't asked her. Though she tried to tell herself that was because the girls' presence had preempted any serious discussions on their part, she doubted that was actually the case. His ardent lovemaking notwithstanding, she guessed, Sam wasn't ready to knit their separate lives back together. He might never be. If so, she'd just have to get used to it.

I'm not sure I could bear it if we turned out to be one of those couples who meet every autumn and do it for old times' sake, she tortured herself. Of course, there'd be compensations. Like the characters in some three-hankie movie, they'd share a heightened consciousness of time's swift passage, erotic detail. Yet they'd miss the daily texture of each other's lives, the comfort of waking up each morning together.

Ironically she realized that the turtle patrol was seasonal, as well. It would be over for another year in August, at the end of the nesting season. Once it had finished, Sam would spend the bulk of his time in Charleston. She wondered how he'd fill the gap its absence would create in his routine. By dating Carolyn, perhaps?

In Sam's opinion, Marcie was quiet, even a little pensive as they transported the girls to the beach for an afternoon swim before driving them into town. Concluding that she was weary from lack of sleep and the late hours they'd kept the night before, he didn't inundate her with questions. Instead, while the ten-year-olds splashed in the surf, thoroughly enjoying the final hours of their weekend vacation on Edisto, he lounged beside her on the beach blanket he'd brought for that purpose and pondered his next move.

He hadn't been terribly surprised, that morning, to see her packing up her things. She needed a lift back to town in order to conduct her interviews. And he was taking the girls. It only made sense for her to ride along. The rub was her corresponding need to get back to New York at some point.

What did he plan to do about it?

If he asked her to stay, she might counter by inviting him to renew their former living arrangement. He doubted he could bring himself to accept. His life in Charleston—with the turtle patrol, his single house that needed renovating and his cartoons to amuse him in addition to paying the bills—was the happiest he'd ever known—if he discounted the empty place at its center.

He'd like to put Marcie back in that place, while giving up none of the above. That is, he would if she could be happy and fulfilled living in South Carolina with him. He sure as hell didn't want to evoke a replay of the past, in which one of them felt frustrated, the other guilty and both were miserable.

All too soon, from Marcie's point of view, it was time to go. Returning to the cottage, they loaded the girls' stuff and Marcie's overnight bag into the Jeep. She took a final picture of Sam and the girls on his front steps and then put away her camera. Before I know it, our time together will be just a memory, she thought. I'll be back in New York, looking at contact sheets, and slides on a light-table, and contemplating emotional damage control.

Pride wouldn't let her make the first move toward an alternative outcome. It was bad enough that, in just a few days, she'd fallen hopelessly in love with Sam again—so much so that she was desperately casting about for ways to test the waters, a formula for reconciling their disparate lifestyles.

The fact that Sam hadn't given her the slightest hint he was doing the same thing gave her a faintly sick feeling in the pit of her stomach. Though they were close again, closer than she'd have dreamed possible after so much time apart, she didn't have a clue where she stood with him. I wish I had the nerve to ask, she thought.

As she was quickly to find out, Shelby lacked any such compunctions. They were about to cross the Ashley River Bridge into the city's historic district when the orphaned ten-year-old leaned her forearms on the back of Sam's seat and posed several rapid-fire questions.

"Are you and Marcie still married, Sam?" she asked. "Do you love each other? Is she going to stay in Charleston now so you can live together?"

Her breath catching as if it had been dragged across a bed of rusty nails, Marcie didn't speak. Beneath the light tan she'd acquired, she could feel her cheeks flushing.

As startled as she, Sam took his time about answering. "Yes to the first question...legally," he replied after a moment. "As you can see, we're good friends. Our future plans are none of your business, Shel."

Seemingly possessed of a healthy sense of self-esteem, Shelby didn't wither at the gentle rebuke. "I was just wondering," she said casually, her blond hair blowing about her freckled face. "I heard Lizzie's mom and Carolyn Deane talking about it."

The news that Sam's sister Georgina and her pal Carolyn had been discussing her and Sam was anything but welcome to Marcie. Whether he realized it or not, it was obvious to her that the simpering brunette had a personal stake in the situation.

Her ire was further provoked when she spotted Carolyn's car in the Herndon drive. They're probably talking about us now, she thought, gritting her teeth. Nothing would please Georgina more...or for that matter, Halette...than to have Sam divorce me and marry Carolyn. I can hardly wait to interview them.

It wasn't long before they were pulling to the curb in front of Dacinda's mansion on the East Battery. "I've got to drop off some stuff at my assistant's to be lettered and inked," Sam told Marcie as she and Shelby got their things out of the Jeep. "Plus run some other errands. But I'll be back in time to have dinner with you all."

After what they'd shared, getting a last look at Sam across Dacinda's exquisitely appointed dinner table wasn't exactly what Marcie had in mind. "I suppose you'll be heading back to Edisto afterward," she murmured, willing him to contradict her.

In the next breath, he did. "Not tonight," he reassured her. "It's my turn for a break. Joe and Tim can handle the patrol in Joe's truck."

A little of the stress that had been building inside her dissipated. Shelby posed the questions I wanted to ask though I wouldn't have put them quite so bluntly, she thought. The prudent thing to do now is wait for answers. "See you later, then," she said, a smile chasing the somber expression from her face.

Waving as he drove off toward the South Battery with his dark hair ruffling in the breeze, Marcie and Shelby toted their bags up Dacinda's front steps and through the false, street-facing door that led onto the piazza.

As they entered the foyer, Dacinda called out to them. "Is that you, Marcie? I presume Shelby's with you."

"Yes to both questions," Marcie answered. About to head up the stairs, she hesitated when Dacinda appeared in the doorway of her favorite yellow-and-white drawing room.

Her hair perfectly coiffed and her blue eyes sparkling, Marcie's mother-in-law looked particularly radiant in a slim, ivory silk dress. "Come join us for a moment," she said to Marcie, giving Shelby a welcoming smile.

Who's *us?* Marcie wondered. In contrast to Dacinda's genteel attire, she was wearing cutoffs and a T-shirt that were ready for the laundry. "Dressed like this?" she asked.

"You look fine...like you've been trompin' around outdoors, that's all. Shelby, take Marcie's duffel bag upstairs for her, will you, dear? And go help Salome in the kitchen. We're goin' to be talkin' grown-up talk."

Marcie's mouth fell open a moment later when she followed Dacinda into the drawing room to find her boss, Glenn Bokaw, sipping a martini in front of its elegant, cream-colored hearth. Clearly amused by her state of shock, he gave her one of his mock salutes.

Well aware Glenn had been Des Whitney's commanding officer during part of the latter's stint in the navy, and that he'd known Dacinda for some time, both through Des and a number of mutual contacts in the field of journalism, she'd had no idea he was planning a trip south. Or that he and her mother-in-law would be getting together. Neither had said a word about it. It was almost as if they hadn't wanted her or Sam to know.

I'm positive Glenn didn't come all the way down here just to check up on how I'm doing with my assignment, Marcie thought. So, what gives? Is it possible Dacinda talked him into making me write about Sam in the hope of getting us back together? Are they in *cahoots?*

"What are you doing here?" she asked.

Like Dacinda, Glenn fairly glowed with well-being. He gave her a contented smile. "It's a long story," he suggested. "Why don't you join us for a drink?"

"Yes, do," Dacinda echoed, linking her arm through his. "We have a lot to talk about."

A martini shaker and several additional glasses stood ready on a piecrust table. It was after 4:00 p.m., and suddenly the idea of a cocktail appealed to Marcie. She had a feeling that maybe she ought to brace herself.

Pouring out a modest portion of ice-cold gin and vermouth and adding a twist of lemon peel with the miniature silver tongs provided for that purpose, she appropriated one of the room's yellow velvet wing chairs. Dacinda and Glenn settled on the butterfly-patterned damask sofa opposite her. They were sitting extremely close together.

They're awfully cozy all of a sudden, Marcie thought. The way Dacinda threaded her arm through his a minute ago...

Before she could complete the thought, Glenn hit her from left field. "You might as well know, Marcie," he said. "My sixty-fifth birthday is coming up in a few weeks. I plan to retire from my position at *Zoom* and move here, to Charleston, just as soon as I'm able."

Marcie stared at him in consternation. "I had no idea you were . . . thinking along those lines. Wh-when will you be leaving the magazine?" she stammered.

Glenn's eyes met Dacinda's. "November first or there-abouts."

Marcie was silent a moment, assessing the consequences. "Any idea who'll be taking your place?" she asked.

"The editorial board will be interviewing candidates, of course. Off the record, Des Whitney has the inside track. He had a successful magazine career, you know, between the time he retired from the navy and signing on here, at the *Gazette*. And he's got the right stuff when it comes to managing people. I'm surprised he didn't mention something."

Recalling Des's comment as he'd kissed her good-night outside Carolyn Deane's apartment, Marcie realized he'd probably wanted to. She hadn't given him the opportunity. "To date, I've spent most of my time on Edisto chasing turtles at your behest," she said a trifle rebelliously. "I don't suppose he's had much of a chance. Glenn, I . . ."

Her boss's Yankee accents were soothing. "I know . . . you'll miss me," he agreed. "As I'll miss you. But you'll like working for Des, Marcie. Compared to me, he's a pussycat."

Against her will, tears stung her eyelids. She really *would* miss Glenn. In addition, he was making the kind of move she'd only begun to contemplate—one she had doubts about whatever perspective she chose to take. "*Zoom* won't be the same without you," she said, "though I admit, working for Des will be the next best thing. I hope you realize I'd never begrudge you happiness. The fact is, I'm pleased if this is what you want to do."

"It is." Taking a sip of his martini, Glenn squeezed Dacinda's hand.

Increasingly aware that, without her knowing it, Glenn and Dacinda had become involved, Marcie focused on a question that was personally significant to her. "I can't help but wonder," she blurted, "won't you miss New York?"

Glenn responded with one of his crinkly smiles. "Not with Dacinda in Charleston."

Again he and Dacinda exchanged a look. This time, Marcie's mother-in-law blushed like a schoolgirl.

Abruptly Marcie got the full picture. "You mean..." she asked in astonishment.

Glenn nodded. "We're getting married just as soon as I can discharge my responsibilities to the magazine. Say you're happy for us."

"Oh, Glenn...Dacinda...*of course* I am!"

Jumping up from her chair so abruptly she almost sloshed her martini on Dacinda's priceless carpet, Marcie set her glass aside to cross the space between them and hug them both. The tears spilled. Within seconds, she and Dacinda were laughing and crying together.

Predictably, it was Dacinda who recovered first. She dabbed daintily at her eyes with a lace handkerchief, which she checked for running makeup. "I trust you'll act equally surprised when we break the news to Sam and his sisters at dinner tonight," she said. "I don't want them to be upset that we told you first."

Shaking her head at the heartwarming miracle of their commitment to each other, and wishing she and Sam could be equally lucky, Marcie assured them she'd do her best.

She spent another ten minutes or so in the drawing room listening as they unveiled their honeymoon plans. Clearly besotted with his catch, Glenn planned to take Dacinda on a round-the-world tour emphasizing the Far East. He wanted to show her the many ports he'd visited as a naval officer, including several in the Philippines, Japan and Australia. They'd be gone three months.

As she showered a short time later and dressed for dinner in a pale pink cotton frock that complemented her hair and lightly tanned complexion, Marcie tried to examine the situation in which she found herself. Now that she knew how close they were, she had an even stronger suspicion that Dacinda had conspired with Glenn to throw her and Sam together. Did she do it because she thinks it'll make Sam happy? she wondered. Or was there another reason? What will happen to Shelby when they go off on their wedding trip?

That night, dinner would be adults only. Given Shelby's willingness to pose awkward questions and her uncanny ability to analyze the adult lives around her, Marcie was glad Salome would be giving the girl her supper in the kitchen and sending her upstairs afterward to watch television in her room.

Halette, Georgina and their husbands had arrived by the time she went back downstairs. Though outwardly they were gracious, as befitted their upbringing at Dacinda's hands, she thought she could detect an undercurrent of animosity in the way they treated her. To them, she was already Sam's ex-wife, she supposed.

"I have to admit I'm a little surprised you're still here," Halette murmured sweetly when they had a moment alone together.

"How's that?" Marcie said, keeping her feelings under wraps.

"Well, it doesn't usually take this long to research a feature, does it? All you have to do is take notes and write down what you see, in addition to gettin' a few quotes...."

Behind Halette's back, Glenn was discreetly shaking his head. He gave Marcie a sympathetic look.

With him watching her, she couldn't help but rise to the occasion. "Actually," she told her sister-in-law, "it's a bit more complicated than that. But I'm almost finished. I just need a couple more interviews...with you and Georgina, to be specific. How about tomorrow morning? Will you be available?"

For once, Halette appeared taken aback. "You want to interview *us?*" she trilled. "Whatever for?"

Marcie shrugged. "You're Sam's sisters. One focus of my story is feminist backlash against his strip. I have marching orders from my editor to find out what the women in his family think about that. If you don't believe me, just ask him."

Halette appeared to consider the idea and reject it. Beckoning Georgina, she explained that Marcie needed to interview them before concluding her research. "She can't return to New York until she talks with us," she said, putting her own spin on the situation. "Is tomorrow mornin' good for you?"

As Carolyn's best friend, Georgina appeared to think the request had merit if it would speed Marcie's departure. "I suppose so," she answered with obvious reluctance. "Why don't we meet here, around 10:00 a.m., on Mother's piazza, if that's all right?"

A moment later, Sam arrived, saving Marcie from further interaction with his sisters. On time for a change, he squeezed her hand in lieu of giving her the hello kiss he'd have preferred.

"You look good enough to eat," he said.

"Thanks. So do you."

Though she immediately focused on him, Marcie didn't fail to catch the less-than-delighted look Halette and Georgina exchanged. It's clear they don't share Dacinda's apparent wish that Sam and I get back together, she thought. Strange, isn't it? I was so sure Dacinda didn't like me, when all along, it seems, she's been pulling for us. Since my arrival last week, I've felt perfectly comfortable with her.

They had just a few minutes to chat before Salome appeared in the connecting doorway to the dining room to announce that dinner was ready. Seated across from her, Sam regarded Marcie thoughtfully as they began with shrimp cocktail. Though he gave no hint of it, he was mulling over the queries Shelby had put to him earlier.

It's hard to believe I gave Carolyn a second look when Red was about to come back into my life, he thought. Of course, there isn't any guarantee I'll be able to keep her there. At some point before she left for New York, he realized, they'd have to talk. Though they'd been so close on the beach some fifteen hours earlier that he'd almost sensed their souls could merge, he didn't mind admitting the idea made him a little nervous.

The shrimp cocktail was followed by oyster soup, roast capon with "dirty" rice, a green salad, black-eyed peas, scalloped corn and fried okra. There was more food than anyone could eat, all of it Salome's scrumptious best.

At last, the clink of cutlery slowed, then stopped altogether. Helped by Wanetta Tomkins, her part-time assistant, Salome cleared away the soiled dinner plates and brought out her pièce de résistance, a raspberry mocha charlotte. The women rolled their eyes as the men groaned audibly and patted the waistbands of their trousers.

Glenn, meanwhile, opened several bottles of champagne that had been cooling in a footed ice bucket beside the buffet. Here it comes, Marcie thought, surreptitiously watching Sam's face. The big announcement.

"Before we start dessert," Glenn said, passing filled glasses to everyone, "I'd like to propose a toast. To our hostess, Dacinda Jeffords...successful newspaperwoman and civic leader, beloved mother, esteemed mother-in-law...not to mention the light of my existence. I hope each and every one of you will share the joy I felt when she agreed to become my wife..."

As he paused to look around the room, several gasps were heard. Marcie did her best to appear surprised as shock, followed by a wave of stocktaking and stunned congratulations, reverberated around the table. She felt a distinct surge of pride when Sam got up and hugged his mother. He was also the first to shake Glenn's hand and bid him welcome to the family.

"I'm really happy for the two of you," he said in a tone that left no doubt the sentiment was genuine. "Mom's needed someone like you, Glenn, for a long, long time. I must say...you guys sure can keep a secret!"

Marcie's boss laughed, giddier with pleasure than she'd ever seen him. "Your mother insisted we tell the family together," he said. "And it's worked out rather well, I think. I just wish we'd thought to borrow a photographer from the *Gazette*. If only you could have seen the looks on your faces..."

With Sam having broken the ice, the rest of the family lined up for hugs and handshakes. At last, everyone returned to their places and Salome's calorie-laden dessert was served. In the excitement, few of the diners did it justice. Glenn in particular scarcely ate a bite as he described the honeymoon plans.

In the discussion that followed, he saw fit to tease Marcie about her fears that he'd miss New York and she'd miss him. "I can promise you the former won't happen," he said, taking Dacinda's hand in his. "As for the latter, Des will likely be taking my place. Plus my assistant, Chuck Morrow, is quitting to pursue his dream of editing a weekly newspaper in western New York state. The number-two slot at *Zoom* will be opening up as well. I'm sure you stand a good chance of landing it, Marcie, if you decide to try for it."

It was the kind of job opportunity she'd been yearning for. Now that it might be about to drop in her lap, she wasn't sure she wanted it. "I don't know, Glenn...." She hesitated, toying with her barely touched dessert. "I'm not at all sure it would be my cup of tea."

Shrugging, he gave her a fatherly smile. "If, like me, you're ready for a change of pace, you could get the advanced degree you want," he advised. "Or write that book you're always talking about. Of course, Des's job at the *Gazette* will likely come open, too. It goes without saying that you're acquainted with the publisher."

I couldn't have laid out the Redhead's options any more neatly if I'd tried for a month of Sundays, Sam thought as he listened quietly but attentively to his future stepfather's remarks. The only thing Glenn neglected to mention is that Marcie's acceptance of a promotion at *Zoom* would probably spoil any chance we have for reconciliation.

As always, he felt enormous guilt, expecting her to accommodate him—in particular, to give up her preferred life-style and place of residence for his. Her alleged fears that Glenn would miss New York, which were probably a metaphor for her own, only exacerbated his sense of culpability.

To complicate things, neither of them was getting any younger. And he continued to want a baby. Ironically, Glenn's suggestion that Marcie pursue her master's degree and/or write a book dovetailed beautifully with a move to Charleston and the demands of motherhood. With the intimate knowledge he'd gained while he and Marcie had lived together, he could imagine her happy with such an existence. The question was, would she consider it? Or was her attachment to life in New York too great?

We have to talk, he thought, his eyes meeting Marcie's for a moment and then refocusing on nothing in particular as their dinner partners moved on to a discussion of where and when the Jeffords-Bokaw nuptials would be held.

Not long afterward, Dacinda signaled that the meal was over. One by one, family members drifted out to the piazza, where the conversation started up again. Apparently willing to accept the idea that their mother's widowhood would end with Glenn, who was both childless and moderately wealthy, Halette and Georgina were pushing the idea of an engagement party at the country club.

"Come walk with me awhile," Sam requested, lacing his fingers through Marcie's as they hung back in the foyer by unspoken mutual consent. "I'd like a few minutes alone with you."

Will he raise the issues I'm longing to discuss? she wondered. Or just chat about nothing in particular and kiss me good-night? "All right," she agreed, deciding to hope for the best.

As they trod the elevated walkway along the seawall beside Charleston Harbor on their way to the shady environs of Battery Park, they held hands but didn't talk much. It was only when they arrived at the park itself that Sam put his arms around her waist and invited her to speak her mind.

"What do you think of my mother's engagement to your boss?" he asked.

The question was an easy one. "I think it's wonderful," she said. "I'd be willing to bet every cent I own that he'll make her happy."

Just then, a blond girl about Shelby's age passed by on roller skates. Sam watched her meditatively for a moment. Then, "What would make *you* happy, Red?" he asked in a low voice.

Having you again, she thought. Not just for a few stolen nights. But forever. Sensing it was time for honesty, she decided to take the risk of saying so.

"Waking up with you every morning," she whispered. "Going to bed with you every night. I'm not quite sure how to arrange it so we wouldn't get in a mess like the one that drove us apart."

"Ah, Red..."

Seconds later, his mouth had covered hers and he was kissing her so lovingly that her heart wanted to break. The kiss lasted almost a full minute, ending only when a couple of teenage boys on skateboards serenaded them with catcalls.

"It's what I want, too, babe," Sam said, tilting her chin with one finger as the boys drifted off to other pursuits. "I never really stopped wanting it, you know. In my opinion, some of the stuff that broke us up was stupid and doesn't have to be repeated. But geography and the demands of your career are another matter. I'm not sure I could stand to move back to New York. Or that I'd be happy with a commuter relationship. Which kind of puts the onus on you. And that's not fair. I don't mind admitting I was all ears when Glenn talked about your various options at the dinner table...."

Aware that any response she made would be seminal in their new relationship, and too seasoned, after everything they'd been through, to make rash promises she couldn't keep, Marcie didn't answer him immediately.

"I, too, found them very interesting," she said at last. "And I don't mean that in a pejorative sense. Glenn knows me well enough to have a pretty good idea of the kind of career changes I might like to make. With so much upheaval in the air and you so deep in my heart, I realize it's time I considered them."

His hopes buoyed instead of dashed, Sam tightened his grip. "If we want to, and I think we do, I don't have the slightest doubt we can make a life that will work for both of us," he said.

Returning to Dacinda's house at a leisurely pace, they discussed her possible choices in more detail. As she talked, one thought building on another, Marcie found herself leaning toward two of them—getting a master's degree *and* writing a book. Perhaps a way can be found to build one on the other, she thought.

"What if I wrote the book as my master's thesis?" she proposed. "To do it, I might have to commute between Charleston and Columbia on a regular basis, with an occasional trip thrown in to New York or Washington."

"Charleston to Columbia isn't much of a jaunt," Sam replied. "As for the other trips you might need to make, I want you to know money wouldn't be an object."

Smiling up at him, Marcie gave him a little squeeze. "You're being awfully sweet to me," she accused.

In deference to her thought processes, which had been proceeding with leaps and bounds, Sam hadn't said very much. Happy and relieved that they were on the same wavelength again, he was still somewhat concerned about asking her to make so many adjustments. He was also worried about how to broach his hopes where Shelby was concerned. The last thing I want is for Marcie to think my desire to make a home for her is my only motive for wanting a reconciliation, he thought.

By the time they entered Dacinda's walled garden, the piazza was deserted. Though Sam's Jeep and Glenn's and Marcie's rental cars were still there, the Mills' and the Herndons' automobiles were absent from the drive. It looks as if my sisters have gone home to conduct a postmortem over the telephone, Sam thought.

"You coming home with me tonight?" he asked, drawing Marcie into his arms beneath a large magnolia tree.

I'd like nothing better, she admitted to herself. Yet she knew she needed time, enough to think her way through the options they'd discussed. It wasn't a function she performed very well in his arms. She also had several early appointments. I can't see myself digging out of Sam's bed to come over here and talk to Georgina and Halette, she thought. Most definitely not!

"Maybe I'd better stay here," she told him gently. "I'm scheduled to interview your mother over breakfast. And your sisters have agreed to drop by around 10:00 a.m."

Though he was disappointed, Sam understood. "I plan to spend Monday night in town, too, because of a Tuesday-morning appointment with my investment analyst," he said. "You're spending it with me. I refuse to negotiate on that point."

Due back in New York on Wednesday afternoon, Marcie was only too happy to say yes. Kissing Sam a lingering good-night, she watched him leave, then turned and went into the house. She was about to head upstairs when she realized to her surprise that she was hungry.

The fact was, she'd eaten very little dinner. I wonder if Salome will forgive me for raiding the refrigerator? she thought, comfortable enough by now in her mother-in-law's East Battery mansion to make a lightning detour in the direction of the kitchen. She was about to push open the swinging door that connected it with the dining room when she realized Glenn and Dacinda had preceded her.

As she hesitated, wondering whether or not she ought to join them, she couldn't help overhearing part of their conversation.

"I'm so glad Sam and Marcie seem to be resolvin' their differences now that we're gettin' married and we'll be gone so much," Dacinda murmured between bites of something. "It'll be better for them. And...hopefully...for Shelby. Georgina offered to have her while we're away. But she doesn't really like the child, I'm afraid. And I can hardly leave her here, with Salome her only baby-sitter."

Abandoning the idea of leftovers, Marcie retreated to her room. Is Sam planning to *adopt* Shelby? she asked herself as she kicked off her shoes and flopped in a brocade easy chair. If so, why didn't he mention it?

Chapter Nine

In the morning, Glenn went jogging with a former navy buddy who lived a few blocks from Dacinda's house. Shelby left early for theatrical tryouts sponsored by the park district. As a result, when Marcie came downstairs and appropriated one of the Chinese Chippendale chairs in Dacinda's dining room, she and her mother-in-law had the breakfast table all to themselves.

Clad in slim, light blue linen slacks and a matching silk T-shirt, Dacinda was already seated in her usual place. She gave Marcie a benevolent smile. "Good mornin', dear," she said with equanimity. "Did you sleep well?"

Too well, Marcie longed to retort. I'd have preferred Sam's light snoring at my elbow. She nodded. "Yes, thanks, Dacinda. And you?"

Not too surprisingly, the older woman's face positively glowed with contentment. "Very well," she replied, the huge diamond Glenn had given her causing fragments of light to dance around the room as she stirred artificial sweetener into her coffee.

Waiting until Salome had served up creamy scrambled eggs, crisp benne biscuits and curried fruit, and they'd each had a chance to fill their plates, Marcie flipped open her reporter's notebook. *I feel a little funny quizzing Dacinda about Sam even if he knows I'm doing it—and approves—* she admitted to herself. *Since it's for a story, and he's given his permission, I suppose it's ethical.*

It continued to bother her that one of the questions she had didn't fit those parameters. She decided to ask it anyway—at the close of the interview.

"Okay if we get started?" she asked.

Dacinda buttered a biscuit. "Fire away. Of course you realize that, where Sam's concerned, I'm prejudiced."

That makes two of us, Marcie thought. *I didn't appreciate him when I had him. But I wouldn't make the same mistake again. In my book, he's the very best.*

"As his mother...someone who's known Sam all his life...how would you describe his attitude toward women?" she asked.

Dacinda gave a delighted laugh. "He likes them!"

Marcie couldn't help grinning, too. "You know what I mean," she protested.

"Actually, I'm not sure I do."

"Well, how does he view us? As intelligent, capable beings who are fully equal to men? Or puzzling, capricious creatures who are always good for a laugh? Dare I say it...as sex objects?"

The older woman tilted her head to one side. "You're askin' me?" she inquired lightly. "*You're* the one who's married to him."

Until she'd sought him out in Charleston, Marcie's marriage to Sam had dwindled to a technicality. Now, thanks to what she suspected was Dacinda's and Glenn's inspired meddling, they had a chance to put things right. "Glenn advised me to describe my, er, connection with Sam for the reader and then set it aside," she explained. "I don't have to tell you that, as a journalist, I have to be objective. My opinion doesn't count."

Dacinda's mouth curved slightly at the mention of her fiancé. "Of course, as your editor, Glenn knows best," she agreed. "Let's see ... I'd have to say Sam views women as equals and treats them that way. I raised him, after all."

She'd raised Halette and Georgina, too—with less success, in Marcie's opinion. Maybe they took after their father. "What else?" she asked.

"I think he sees them as amusing. Capable. Sexy. And somewhat mysterious. He once told me he thought there should be a certain amount of mystery between the sexes. That's healthy, don't you think?"

Limiting her response to a practiced half shrug that prevented her subjects from turning the tables and interviewing *her,* Marcie wrote.

"If Sam sees women as equals, why don't feminists like 'Male Animal'?" she asked.

Dacinda took a meditative sip of her coffee. "Maybe they don't understand it," she speculated. "Or else they're hell-bent on maintaining political correctness, and so miss the point. It's just my opinion, of course. But I don't see 'Male Animal' as straight social commentary. It's humor. It points out truth by exaggeration."

Agreeing, Marcie didn't concur aloud. "Could you explain that a bit?" she asked.

Dacinda was silent a moment. "Well, misunderstandin' is one of the underpinnin's of humor. As I see it, 'Male Animal' is about the funny, ironic situations that arise from miscommunication between the sexes. Mystery carried to extremes, you might say. And the fumbles that result. In an underlyin' way, I also think it chronicles women's battle for equality. Some of Sam's characters are all for it. Others are fightin' a rearguard action.

"Sam has hinted more than once that he doesn't always share the confusion about women Jake and his male buddies express. Or agree with them. He just portrays what some men think...zeroin' in on what's funny and ironic about their opinions. The more radical feminists who've bashed his strip fail to see that, I think."

In accord with her mother-in-law's thoughtful, articulate analysis, Marcie wondered why she and Dacinda had failed to become friends earlier. Maybe her status as a lady of the old school who also happened to be a professional powerhouse had something to do with it, she thought as she scribbled. It's possible I resented her for being successful in so many areas, when her kind of success was exactly what I wanted.

Of course she hadn't wanted to live without a permanent man in her life. Despite her many beaux, Dacinda had done that since Sam was in grade school. It was time she married again.

"Quite a few of Sam's themes involve men's problems with their wives' and girlfriends' careers," she noted. "As the first working woman in Sam's life, how do you think he felt about your job? Especially when he was small?"

The food on Dacinda's plate cooled as her blue eyes gazed down the years. "He resented it at times, I suppose," she admitted with commendable honesty. "Particularly at first. When his father died, Sam was just eight years old. Halette was ten, Georgina twelve. I had three choices. Sell the *Gazette,* entrust it to someone else to run or run it myself. Bein' a woman of conviction, I chose to run it. I spent a lot of time at the paper durin' those early days. The learnin' curve was very steep."

Writing silently, Marcie waited.

"I remember one evenin' when I was free for a change, Sam and I sat on the piazza until well after dark," Dacinda added. "He'd asked me why I had to work, and I'd answered that I was doin' it so he and his sisters could continue to live in this big, old house, and go to college someday. Those weren't the only reasons, though, and we both knew it. So I tried to explain about the satisfaction part of workin'... the kind of self-affirmation both men and women need, and get, from their careers. Lookin' back, maybe I flatter myself. But I think he understood."

Neither of them spoke for a moment as a light breeze off the harbor stirred the dining room curtains. It's true, Marcie thought. Sam never resented my working. Just the fact that I wouldn't move to South Carolina. Or go on leave long enough to have a baby. Of course he wanted me to cook for him. Sew on buttons, that kind of thing. In retrospect, I don't think domesticity was really the issue. Maybe it was just a delayed reaction to Dacinda's career... an attack of childhood resentment that got misplaced.

"Tell me how you viewed Sam's relationships with women historically," she said at last, aware she was asking partly out of a desire to hear her mother-in-law's opinion of their relationship.

Dacinda nodded as if she found the question an easy one. "I guess you could say he suffered the usual pangs of puppy love, the requisite bumps and bruises to his ego that we all must face," she related. "As I recall, his first confrontation with the opposite sex involved a young woman named Sabrina Pomfret, who happened to be his second-grade teacher. One afternoon shortly before dinnertime, he marched out of the house with two candy bars clutched in a grubby fist and a look of sheer determination on his face. Curious, I followed, though I was careful to keep my distance.

"It turned out that he was headed for Miss Pomfret's house. After spendin' a few minutes on her front porch, he started back, cryin'. When I kind of fell into step with him and asked what was wrong, he told me he'd proposed marriage to her through the screen door. The candy bars had been intended as an engagement present. He was mortally embarrassed when her fiancé walked up behind her in his undershorts and laughed at him."

Though she smiled at Dacinda's account, Marcie felt sympathy, as well. She'd caught a glimpse of the male vulnerability to rejection that surfaced now and then in Sam's strip. Thanks to the insight her mother-in-law had provided, she thought she understood it a little better.

"And after that?" she prompted.

Again Dacinda shrugged. "The usual schoolboy crushes. He went steady a couple of times in high school . . . played the field in college. Though he continued to date after he moved to New York, there wasn't anyone serious in his life that I knew about . . . until you came along."

Abruptly, silence filled Dacinda's pleasant dining room. Here it comes, Marcie thought. I can't blame her for asking. *I* would, in her place.

"Since you've been kind enough to give me an openin', I'm goin' to take it," Dacinda said after a moment's hesitation, declining to phrase her appeal for information as a question. "Two years is a long time for people who love each other to live apart. Just for the record, I'd like to say how happy I am that you and Sam seem to be workin' out your differences."

Though their talk the night before had been anything but conclusive, Sam had been up-front about wanting what she wanted. He'd expressed his faith that they could make a go of things. Surely Dacinda deserved to hear that much.

"I'd rather you didn't pass this along to anyone except your coconspirator," she said. "But Sam and I have been talking reconciliation. We haven't worked out the details yet...."

Marcie's mother-in-law reached across the table to squeeze her hand. "But that's wonderful, darlin'," she exclaimed. "I'm not sure I know what you mean by 'coconspirator,' though."

The pretention caused Marcie to laugh outright. "Oh...I think you do," she asserted. "Given your relationship with Glenn, you can't really expect me to believe you had nothing to do with my assignment. Your fingerprints are all over it."

Dacinda had the grace to blush. "What if they are?" she retorted. "I told Glenn it was high time you and Sam got another look at each other, and he agreed it was a fine idea. One thing led to another. Your assignment was the upshot. I don't hear you cryin' foul, dear heart."

Marcie couldn't help dimpling at her own expense. As far as she was concerned, the interview was over. She set her notebook aside. "Why would I do that," she said, "when I got exactly what I wanted? The fact of the matter is, I should be thanking you."

Though Sam's sisters would be arriving at any minute and Marcie had planned to phone a female professor at the college where Sam had been egged several weeks earlier before meeting with them, she remained seated at the table with her mother-in-law, outlining the choices she and Sam faced. At last they'd said everything there was to say. Marcie couldn't put off stating the personal question that was on her mind any longer.

"I wonder if I could ask you about something I haven't had the gumption to discuss with Sam yet?" she remarked.

Her mother-in-law's poise was seamless. "Be my guest."

"Actually, it's about Shelby. I gather she's with you on a temporary basis. What kind of future do you envision for her?"

Dacinda regarded her silently for a moment. But though she labeled it confidential, she didn't hesitate to provide the information Marcie wanted.

"Shelby's mother is a drug addict livin' in California," she revealed. "She doesn't want the girl. She signed away her parental rights years ago. Meanwhile, Sam and Shelby's father, Jack, were best friends, goin' back to their high school days. He loves Shelby as if she were his own. Now that Jack's gone, he wants to adopt her. And it's obvious she wants that, too, though he hasn't spoken to her about it yet. Because of his single life-style and the fact that he's...officially...in the process of a divorce, he's run into problems. The child welfare people and the court are lookin' at other options in her case."

Marcie didn't respond as she considered the ramifications of what Dacinda had told her. She hadn't met Jack during the five years of her marriage because he'd worked out of Key West, Florida, during that period and she didn't know much about him. Why hasn't Sam discussed any of this with me? she wondered. Is he afraid I'll run from the responsibility? Or does he have another, less acceptable reason for his silence on the subject? If she let it, she realized, the news about his desire to adopt Shelby could add up to ulterior motives where his eagerness to save their marriage was concerned.

That was also true in Dacinda's case.

With unerring accuracy, Marcie's mother-in-law targeted what was in her thoughts. "I'm eager for you and Sam to put your marriage back together because I want to see him happy," she said. "And I don't think he *has* been, without you, no matter how carefree his life may have seemed to the casual observer. But you're right...I do have another purpose for wantin' to smooth out your differences. I just want you to realize it's not the most important one."

Employing an information-gathering technique that had served her well in the past, Marcie drew Dacinda out with her silence.

"You seem to get on well with children," the older woman added, obliging her with a more detailed explanation. "If you and Sam reconciled...and both of you wanted Shelby...her adoption would go forward without a hitch."

I like Shelby despite her precocious, outspoken ways and uncomfortable habit of reading people with devastating accuracy, Marcie thought. Maybe even because of them. At her age, I wasn't so very different. Still, she knew resolving the geographical problems she and Sam faced, not to mention making a go of marriage on their second try, would be a tall order without signing on for instant motherhood.

"I believe you when you say providing for Shelby isn't your only concern," she told Dacinda, reluctant to air her feelings about the girl since she wasn't completely certain of them yet. "I just hope it isn't Sam's."

Gazing past her, Dacinda smiled as Glenn entered the room, dripping sweat in shorts and a T-shirt. "Why don't you ask him?" she suggested, lifting her face for her fiancé's kiss.

* * *

While Marcie was waiting for Halette and Georgina to arrive, she went into Dacinda's study and phoned the feminist professor who'd attended Sam's commencement speech. To her disappointment, the woman had toned down her scathing opinions in the weeks following his talk. What they'd gained in fairness and moderation, they'd lost in reader interest. Questions about what had occasioned the shift didn't get Marcie to first base.

As alike as two peas in a pod, Sam's slim, dark-haired sisters were waiting for her on the piazza when she emerged. About to go out and join them, she hesitated when she realized they were talking about her and Sam.

"Marcie sure messed things up by showin' up when she did," Georgina was saying. "When Sam took Carolyn along on that trip to Atlanta last month, I thought they were all set. Now Marcie's been stayin' out at Edisto and he's all lovey-dovey with her. Carolyn came over to my house in tears yesterday. I tell you, she's devastated."

Listening from her position in the cool, shadowed hallway just inside Dacinda's front door, Marcie pushed down the wave of nausea that rose in her stomach. So what if Sam and Carolyn had taken a trip together? It was possible nothing happened between them. Even if it had . . . it qualified as history, not a current event. Sam and I were legally separated when it happened, she told herself. We'll talk about it, lay the issue to rest.

She was a professional journalist. That meant she could interview anyone, no matter how much she disliked them. Or how embarrassed she felt. Fiercely reminding herself of that fact, she stepped out on the piazza, smiled sweetly and started ticking off her questions.

* * *

Not due at Sam's house until 2:00 p.m., and too restless to hang around Dacinda's house following her interview with Sam's sisters, Marcie decided to do a little window-shopping along King Street, which was lined with antique and specialty shops. Around lunchtime, she picked up a copy of the *Gazette* and sought out a bakery/tearoom for a bite to eat. After placing her order for she-crab soup and a croissant, she turned to Sam's cartoon first.

In that day's strip, one of Jake's married friends was telling his barroom buddies how his wife was training him to pick up after himself. She was putting his candy wrappers, beer cans, dirty socks and the like in his briefcase instead of disposing of them for him. During a recent business meeting, he'd reached into it and pulled out the remains of an ice-cream bar instead of the report he wanted.

"Why *can't* she pick up after me?" the misunderstood husband demanded to a chorus of sympathetic looks. "What does she think I am anyway...a grown man?"

For once, instead of grimacing, Marcie found her mouth relaxing into a smile. Sam had subtly switched points of view. Though the speaker was still grousing about the woman in his life, and drawing a chuckle from the reader for it, he'd acknowledged that—occasionally—female complaints were justified. Though personally he might not be any more inclined to pick up after himself than he'd been before, the man who was still Marcie's legal mate had registered an opposing viewpoint. There was definitely hope.

While Marcie had wandered through the city's antique district, Halette and Georgina had driven to the latter's house and changed into their swimming suits. Now, they drank ice tea and smoked mentholated cigarettes on identical chaise longues beside the Herdons' swimming pool. Ostensibly, they were watching Lizzie, Shelby and several neighborhood children splash in the water.

In reality, they were plotting. "The surprise birthday party is a fabulous idea," Georgina was saying. "It's goin' to be hard, though, gettin' Carolyn to cooperate."

Her manner a trifle bored, Halette shrugged. "What choice does she have? If she doesn't play along, she'll lose him. It's that simple. Sam needs a wife to adopt Shelby. And he likes Carolyn. If he's furious at her, he'll get over it. They'll be datin' again within a few months."

Though she did her best to kill time, Marcie arrived at Sam's house a good half hour early. Built in classic Charleston style, it was situated on Tradd Street in the heart of the historic district. As she parked her rental car at the curb and gazed up at it, she remarked to herself that it had "good bones." At the same time, she could see that it needed a lot of work. Its mellow old brick fairly cried out for sandblasting to restore its original rosy glow. Likewise, the woodwork was in desperate need of paint.

Careful not to jump to any conclusions about the future, though she knew Sam cared about her and all the signs were favorable, Marcie couldn't help picturing herself in jeans and an old shirt, wielding a paintbrush on her days off. Is it really possible that I'll be living here in the not-too-distant future? she wondered, tempted to pinch herself as she mounted a narrow set of street-facing steps and opened the unlocked, colonial-style door that led to the piazza. So much has changed so quickly after so much loneliness.

Though her head was spinning with daydreams, she hadn't fully confronted what such an outcome would mean in practical terms. It would shake up my life at the foundation, she realized, rapping lightly on the screen door. I'd have to consider the possibilities Glenn outlined at dinner last night, probably choose one of them. She had to admit that, given her feelings for Sam, refusing to adapt simply wasn't an option.

On the phone in his office, a temporary conversion of his formal dining room, Sam hollered for her to come in. Barefoot and minimally clad in wrinkled khaki shorts, he'd been cleaning in anticipation of her visit. An armload of towels and dirty clothes he'd probably collected from various points around the house adorned the seat of an otherwise empty swivel chair. Unrelieved of its contents, a dustpan waited to be emptied.

Marcie smiled even as she shook her head. Sam might be messy—cavalier about his life-style to the point of sloppiness. But he was the man for her. How could she have failed to appreciate such a salient point? Instead of fighting over the laundry and dirty dishes left lying about, they could hire a housekeeper. With their combined earnings, they wouldn't feel the pinch.

A moment later, he concluded his phone call and put down the receiver. Grinning a bit sheepishly at being caught with his preparations for her arrival half-finished, he held out his arms. All thought of decision making fled as Marcie went into them. How good it was to belong to him again! To know without *having* to be told that they had a future, and would spend the night together. Deliberately inhaling in his scent as she nestled closer, she buried her face against his neck.

She was sniffing him again. Aroused as always by her sensuousness, Sam tugged her closer still, crushing the soft mounds of her breasts against him. How had he managed, without her love, to be sustained? Survived the terrible deprivation of not holding her in his arms? Perfect as his life was now in so many ways, without her it sang of emptiness.

On Edisto and in the park the night before, they'd merged. Become one person while maintaining the erotic tension of their separateness. Now it was happening again. As their kiss deepened, and Sam stroked the muscles of her back and buttocks through the fabric of her shirt and shorts, Marcie knew the state or city she resided in didn't matter. With Sam, wherever he was, she was exactly where she belonged.

We'll spend the afternoon in bed, she promised herself, pressing closer still. While away the hours napping and making love to each other. First, she wanted to see his house. Knowing it as intimately as possible would serve as a kind of lightning rod, grounding her in their love for each other.

Incredibly, he understood. "C'mon," he murmured, drawing back a little though he continued to maintain his hold on her. "I'll show you around. Don't expect anything fancy. I've been batching it here since we split up and the place shows it. I don't mind admitting it needs a woman's touch."

Purchased below market value because it needed so much work, Sam's house had endless possibilities. With its wood floors refinished and gleaming, the right wallpaper, draperies and furniture, Marcie believed, his high-ceilinged drawing room easily would be the rival of Dacinda's. Similarly, though its countertops were covered with pockmarked linoleum, and the classic lines of its cupboards were obscured by multiple coats of chipped, yellowing paint, Sam's kitchen was a dream just waiting to materialize. With plenty of elbow grease and imagination, plus some new appliances, it would be worthy of the glossiest magazine pages.

I can't wait to get started, she thought, her native enthusiasm and Sam's affectionate presence at her elbow overcoming any fear she might have had about getting in too deep emotionally before he'd stated a firm commitment to her.

The house also boasted a breakfast room and a library, where Sam's collection of books was piled haphazardly on perhaps a quarter of its built-in shelves. Extensive square footage in the former slave quarters, which extended in a wing from the main part of the house and faced the rear yard, could be converted to a family room, several guest suites and enough office space for both of them.

Returning to the house proper, they headed upstairs. There were five original bedrooms, one of them perfect for a nursery. As she contemplated the possibility, a half-formed idea popped into her head, causing her to frown slightly. Had she been missing something? A moment later, it eluded her as Sam led the way into the master suite.

How many times she'd tried to picture him there, and never gotten it right. Despite her best efforts, she hadn't been able to envision the way the large, airy space would dwarf the armoire she remembered, his unmade double bed. Or fully appreciate how it would feel to be standing there in its open doorway, on the cusp of making love to him.

"I was going to put on fresh sheets for us," he confessed, lightly massaging her nape beneath her tousled red curls. "But the time got away from me. For one thing, I had at least two dozen phone calls...."

He'd always been prone to exaggeration. Rising slightly on tiptoe, Marcie kissed his cheek. "It's not a problem," she whispered. "We don't need them. We'd just mess them up anyway."

The mutuality of their need rising in a flood, Sam unsnapped the waistband of her shorts and dragged down their zipper tab. Wriggling out of them, she pulled her yellow cotton T-shirt unceremoniously over her head. Seconds later, his shorts and her lacy, minimal underwear lay in a heap with her outer garments on the floor. Skin to skin, her nipples tightening against the hairy maze that covered his chest, they explored each other.

I won't let her go again, Sam thought, leading her toward the bed so he could luxuriate in her sweetness length for length. Whatever it takes, we'll do it, even if that means frequent flyer status for both of us.

What he wanted, though, was more traditional than that. In his heart of hearts, he wanted one life, in which they got up together every morning and went to bed together every night. One roof over their heads. Most particularly he wanted Marcie to have his baby. Was it possible she wanted the same things? That she'd agree to stop taking her birth-control pills once they'd firmed up the details? Just the thought of his infant son or daughter growing beneath her heart was enough to fire his imagination.

In theory, at least, both of them had wanted to frolic—to draw out the sweet initiation of their lovemaking for as many languorous moments as possible before jettisoning the last of their control. Now his longing to be inside her was unruly and deep.

Her bright head on his rumpled pillowcase, Marcie yearned for the same thing. "Sam . . . come into me," she begged, inviting him with open thighs as she drew him even more intimately into her embrace.

He didn't need a second invitation. Fitting himself to the moist aperture within her velvet folds, he slid lovingly inside, then held them motionless for several seconds while he recovered himself. At last, it was all right to move.

Catching his rhythm with a facility born of their history together and matching it flawlessly with hers, Marcie let waves of sensation wash over her. Meanwhile, Sam rode high to achieve maximum impact.

What they were doing couldn't have been more physical. Yet in a way that defied rational interpretation, it knit body and soul together. In their communion, they'd become a single, rapturous unit, something more than the sum of their separate selves. The bonding and reintegration that had begun on her first night in Charleston was achingly complete.

Sam . . . Sam . . . I love you so much! she blurted, uncertain whether she'd voiced the words or if she'd simply articulated them in her head.

Floodgates quivered on the verge of bursting as he answered, his voice nasal and raspy, increasingly distorted as his passion mounted. "Ah, Red . . . I love you, too. . . ."

There was no further need for caution, not even in her secret thoughts. Her most wanton, vulnerable self was safe with him. Her lips parted and her breathing intensified as he made contact with the nub of her desire with each downward stroke.

With a little jolt that placed control beyond her reach, she quickened to his touch. Ripple upon ripple, beginning at a single point of arousal, a warm pool of sensation widened until it threatened to encompass her entire being. Trembling with urgency, she let it spill over. Spasms of pleasure shook her, spreading heat, an exquisite sheen of gooseflesh as her feet clung to the mattress for purchase.

Attuned to her response with every iota of concentration he possessed, Sam was suddenly freed of responsibility. Driving toward his own release, he followed in seconds. Out of their heads, they swam in ecstasy together.

At last they quieted. His body still alive, still tingling, Sam collapsed against her, pressing her into the mattress. Several minutes passed. Finally, rolling onto his side, he drew Marcie's head against his shoulder. She yawned and snuggled closer. Each time they were together, it seemed, the fit improved. As a mockingbird warbled in the moss-draped oak outside his window and the bell of St. Michael's chimed the hour, they drifted in their contentment, eventually falling asleep.

They still had a great deal to talk about. Nudged back to awareness sometime later by a freshening breeze and the clamor of homebound traffic, they kissed and rearranged themselves.

"So... " Sam murmured tenderly, trying not to betray his trepidation. "Where do we start?"

She didn't need a game plan to interpret the question. Nor did she have any trouble guessing how sensitive the subject was for him. "By settling on a place where we can live together," she answered promptly. "One where we can make a life for ourselves. And each other."

His silence warned her that she'd have to state her preference first. If I said "New York," would he go along with it? she wondered. But it was only a passing thought. Since their time together on Edisto, she'd been moving steadily in another direction. The options Glenn had outlined at the dinner table the night before had only helped to confirm that movement.

"What about here, in Charleston?" she asked.

Though his heart leapt, Sam hesitated before answering. "You know how much that would please me," he admitted after a moment. "But... what about your job? And your devotion to life in the big city?"

In response, Marcie restated the choices Glenn had posed. True . . . she still loved New York. But not as much as she loved him. Unsure what she would do professionally, she was able to tell him with complete honesty that she was no longer wedded to a magazine career.

"Des's job at the *Gazette* sounds interesting," she said. "But it might not give me enough freedom in relation to your work. Maybe it *is* time I thought about getting an advanced degree. And writing the book about politics and the media I've been considering. Of course, if Shelby came to live with us . . ."

At the mention of his and Dacinda's youthful protégée, Sam gave her a searching look. "My mother told you about my wanting to adopt her, didn't she?" he asked. "I was going to, I swear. I just couldn't think of a way to break the news that wouldn't make it seem as if I had an ulterior motive for courting you again. I promise you, Red . . . that just isn't so."

Affectionately Marcie bussed him on the cheek. "I know it's not," she reassured him. "I'll admit I'm not used to the idea of mothering a ten-year-old yet. But I like Shelby a lot. And it's growing on me. I just need time to get it in perspective."

Overwhelmed with gratitude that they could discuss the orphaned girl's future so openly and positively, without that discussion threatening their own future, Sam returned her kiss with good measure. "That's all I could possibly ask," he told her.

As the afternoon shadows lengthened, they talked of other things, foremost among them their shared reluctance to part, even for a few months while Marcie worked out the details of moving and her resignation from the *Zoom* staff. Unfortunately, magazines worked several months ahead. Six weeks' notice might not be enough.

She'd also have to pack up her possessions, sort through the pack-rat accumulation of several years and dispose of the nonessentials. Despite those exigencies, she could return in the meantime for a visit.

Having been granted a boon that exceeded his fondest hopes, Sam was disposed to be cooperative. Still, impatience had him by the throat. "Don't be surprised if I turn up in Manhattan in the meantime," he warned later that evening as they rocked gently on his porch swing with his arm about her shoulders. "Now that we've made our plans, spending even a few days without you is asking too much."

Marcie couldn't have agreed more. Happier than she'd dreamed possible when her plane had touched down at Charleston Airport less than a week earlier, she was loath to disturb the flow of good feeling between them. Yet she didn't want any clouds on their horizon.

"I hope you won't misunderstand," she said. "But there's something I need to ask. Before I do, I'd just like to say we'll only have this discussion once. I promise not to bring it up again."

Instantly wary, though he didn't have a clue what she was talking about, Sam invited her to go ahead.

"It has to do with Carolyn," she said. "This morning, at your mother's house, I overheard your sisters discussing a trip you took to Atlanta with her. Would you mind, um, telling me what that was about?"

Though he felt embarrassment and distress over his association with the clinging brunette, Sam had nothing to hide. "In other words, you're asking if I slept with her," he clarified.

Marcie nodded.

"The answer's yes...in the technical sense that we shared a hotel bed. I was lonely. With the deadline we'd set for divorcing just around the corner, I thought you and I were finished. I quickly found out Carolyn wasn't an adequate cure for my loneliness. The fact is, taking that trip to Atlanta with her only made it worse. You might not believe me, but we never had sex. I couldn't go through with it." He paused. "Want to know why?"

Her voice barely above a whisper, Marcie answered in the affirmative.

"Because she wasn't you."

"Oh, Sam..." Flinging both arms around him, she gave him a squeeze that set the swing to rocking erratically. "I love you so much," she exclaimed. "Let's make a pact to start fresh. As far as I'm concerned, the past didn't happen except to teach us."

Chapter Ten

Three weeks later, Marcie's piece about Sam was "in the can"—a colorful, balanced, essentially positive essay that had won high praise from Glenn for its fairness and reader interest. Well into her next, New-York-based assignment, which would be among her last as a *Zoom* staff writer, she was at Fortunoff jewelers, buying the man she loved a birthday present.

After spending several lunch hours shopping her favorite haunts, she'd finally found the perfect gift for him, a solid-gold tie tack shaped like a turtle. In her opinion, it greatly resembled a loggerhead, though it could have been a Kemp's Ridley or a leatherback, for all she knew. As she presented her credit card at the cash register, her head was filled with visions of her stay on Edisto—breeze-swept breakers, Shelby and Lizzie chasing a wriggling mass of newly hatched turtles, Sam naked on the moonlit stretch of channel beyond Jeremy Inlet, making slow, passionate love to her.

He'd be thirty-eight on Wednesday. No longer young in the sense of being immature, but not yet middle-aged, he was a man in a million—smart, funny and capable of great tenderness. Though they'd talked about how nice it would be if she could spend his birthday with him, he didn't expect her to. Instead, he'd declared that having her permanently once she'd rearranged her life would be enough.

Meanwhile, they'd planned for her to visit Labor Day weekend. Excited at the prospect of seeing him far sooner than that, she'd been scrupulously careful during their many phone conversations not to mention the birthday party being organized in his honor, or say anything about juggling her schedule so she could attend.

He's going to be caught totally off guard when everyone yells "Surprise!" she thought. Positively stunned when *I* turn up. Well, he won't be the only one to confront the unexpected. As a result of the way they'd treated her during her recent visit to Charleston, she'd been nothing short of astonished when Halette Mills had phoned to extend the invitation.

"Since you and Sam seem to be on the mend, we thought he'd want you there," the younger of Sam's two sisters had announced in her offhand way, scrupulously avoiding any claim that she or Georgina would share his pleasure in her company. Marcie supposed it was too much to ask that they hadn't invited Carolyn, too. Well, if they had, she could weather it.

The invitation was a start if she and Sam's sisters were ever to feel comfortable around each other. Since, with her move to Charleston at the end of September, they'd be living in close proximity for the first time since her marriage to Sam five years earlier, they might as well try. They'd bump into each other on street corners, see each other regularly on holidays.

No doubt Dacinda was involved in their decision to include me, Marcie speculated as she tucked Sam's gift-wrapped package into her purse and continued her midday stroll up Fifth Avenue. After all she's done for me, the least I can do is forgive Halette and Georgina for preferring Carolyn. As the hands-down winner in my contest with the egregious Ms. Deane, I can afford to be generous.

Though it had been a hot, muggy week, with baking sidewalks and sweltering temperatures, that afternoon the Big Apple's weather was mild and sunny, the air almost effervescent. It felt good just to be alive. I still love New York, Marcie admitted with a twinge of nostalgia. Yet, without Sam to share it, the city's a desert.

In addition to relocating and helping renovate Sam's handsome old single house in the fall, she'd have other irons in the fire. As soon as possible, she planned to enroll in a university-without-walls, start outlining her proposed book. If it was scholarly enough and managed to break new ground, it might serve as a master's thesis. Maybe even a doctoral dissertation.

She'd also write the occasional piece for Des when he took over at *Zoom*. Pleased he'd asked, she expected the free-lance assignments would involve some traveling, an occasional visit to New York if she chose. Admitting he'd planned to court Marcie if and when she was free, Des had remained a good friend to both of them. On learning of their reconciliation, he'd graciously wished them all happiness.

Since her return to New York, the idea of adopting Shelby had gained in appeal. Sam and I won't have the free run of the house for our lovemaking with her underfoot, she realized philosophically as she boarded a bus for the return trip to her office. But then, I want to have Sam's baby before I get much older. So we'll be parents anyway. We'll have to learn to be more circumspect.

A moment later, her thoughts zigzagged in an unexpected direction. Those condoms I took with me to South Carolina, she thought. We didn't use them! I could already be pregnant.

During the early years of their marriage, she'd been on the birth-control pill. He must have assumed I still was, or he'd have used protection, she reasoned, letting a half-thrilled, half-helpless shudder wash over her. *She'd* known better. How could she have "forgotten"—not once but on three separate occasions? The only possible explanation is that I *wanted* to forget, Marcie thought. Apparently my subconscious was doing everything it could to make sure we stayed together.

Getting off the bus a half block from her building and taking an elevator to her sixth-floor office, Marcie did some swift mental calculations. It's very likely that I *am* pregnant, she thought. I don't have anything resembling morning sickness. In fact, I feel wonderful. But my period's usually so regular. And it's already a week late.

What would Sam say when she told him? Picturing his utter astonishment and the elation that would surely follow it, Marcie almost bumped into Glenn outside his office.

"Careful," Dacinda's husband-to-be teased, steadying her with a fatherly hand. "People who are consumed by love tend to be accident-prone."

Excitement spilling over at her discovery, she tossed her head. "You ought to know," she retorted. "Besides, some accidents are positive ones!"

By the time she arrived in Charleston on the morning of Sam's party, Marcie knew for a fact that, whether or not they adopted Shelby, she and Sam would be parents in early March. Her obstetrician-gynecologist had told her so. In the interim, the thrill she'd felt that afternoon on the bus when she'd realized she would have Sam's baby had ripened into deep happiness. Her sense of helplessness had metamorphosed into a perception of flowing at one with the mysteries of existence. Instead of an individual focused on her own myopic concerns, she was a link in the chain of life itself.

If only her hormones weren't in such an uproarious state. Though she still hadn't experienced much in the way of morning sickness, all she had to do was watch a sentimental commercial on television or read a snatch of greeting-card verse and she'd burst into tears. With just a few weeks of motherhood under her belt, she'd become an emotional yo-yo.

She hadn't told Sam about the baby yet, perferring to do so in person when they were alone after his birthday party. In the meantime, I'll have to keep a tight rein on my feelings, she thought as she got off the plane and waved to Dacinda, who'd come to meet her at the airport. I don't want Sam to think I've become a basket case.

Greeting her with a fond hug in the airport terminal, Dacinda remarked on her glowing appearance. "Reconcilin' with Sam has had a positive effect on you, I see," she said as they turned and headed for the car.

Though she did her best to suppress them, tears of pleasure welled up in Marcie's eyes all out of proportion to the compliment. "You can say that again," she responded tremulously.

Dacinda gave her a fond smile. "I might just. Seriously, I'd like to say how pleased I am that you could make it. This'll be Sam's first surprise birthday party ever. And I have a feelin' you're the surprise he'll like best."

Agreed to between them on the phone a few days earlier, the plan was for Marcie to remain out of sight at Dacinda's until it was time to congregate at Sam's with the other party guests. "He'll be comin' in to take me out to dinner... or so he thinks," the older woman had confided. "And go home first to change his clothes. Sam's a dutiful son. When I ask him out to dinner, he usually accepts if his schedule permits. We figured it was the best way to gain his cooperation."

As Marcie got out of Dacinda's car in the courtyard of the latter's East Battery mansion and went inside to sip ice tea with her in its fan-cooled drawing room, Halette and Georgina were busy transporting party supplies, food and drink to Sam's place in the Herndons' station wagon. Heavily laden, they used a spare key they'd borrowed from Dacinda to let themselves in.

They disposed of the makings for punch and several bags of ice cubes first, cramming them into Sam's less-than-orderly refrigerator. "It seems a shame to waste all this food... particularly the cake," Georgina complained as they set out on his paper-tablecloth-bedecked worktable an array of hors d'oeuvres, an empty punch bowl and the bakery confection of which she spoke. "I don't suppose anyone will want it after the denouement."

Halette gave her a disparaging look. "After all these years, you still talk like a literature major," she accused. "As for this stuff, you're welcome to take it home if you want. Lizzie and Todd and Jim can dispose of it. Or you can feed it to the dog, for all I care. You know we have to make this look good. If we don't, Marcie won't buy our innocence. Neither will Mother. And *that* would be a disaster of the first order."

By prearrangement with Carolyn, they left the front door unlocked when they went home to change. Parking her car a few blocks to the east, down a side alley where Sam wouldn't be likely to see it, Marcie's erstwhile rival approached the house a short time later.

Like her friends, she didn't show up empty-handed. Slipping into the front hall after glancing nervously about to make sure she wasn't being observed, Carolyn went directly upstairs. Her facial expression betrayed strong misgivings as she followed Halette's instructions.

Sam had been on the road for about ten minutes by the time the first party guests began arriving at his place to gossip, nibble hors d'oeuvres and inspect the latest cartoon on his drawing board.

Among them were Marcie, Shelby and Dacinda. Gravitating toward each other like the twin halves of an offended mollusk's shell, Lizzie and Shelby retreated to an unobtrusive corner, where they proceeded to stuff themselves with cashews. Waving everyone inside as quickly as possible, Halette and Georgina made a point of reminding each new arrival that surprise was of the essence.

For once Carolyn hadn't materialized. Is it possible they didn't invite her out of deference to me? Marcie thought. Maybe we ought to call the *Guinness Book of World Records!*

Smiling as she linked arms with Marcie, Dacinda took advantage of the opportunity to introduce her around. They chatted with a number of Sam's former high school classmates, the pleasant young man who inked his cartoon, assorted aunts, uncles, cousins and fishing buddies. Marcie was delighted to learn that a nephew of the infamous Miss Pomfret, to whom Sam had proposed when he was in the second grade, had made the guest list.

A few of the people she met had attended her wedding to Sam in New York five years earlier. She supposed most had heard about their breakup. Now that they'd patched up their differences, his friends and relatives seemed to know that, too. Though the situation could easily have been an awkward one, it wasn't. Their gracious Charleston manners fully in evidence, Sam's birthday guests simply remarked how good it was to see her, and promised to be in touch once she took up residence.

As the hour of Sam's arrival approached, his office was filled to bursting. Posting her best friend, Sallie Chambers, just inside the front door to watch for his Jeep, Halette all but closed the heavy wooden pocket doors that separated Sam's office from the hall and reiterated the guests' marching orders.

"When I flip y'all the high sign, I want absolute silence in this room," she said. "Not a whisper. Not a giggle. Particularly not a chair scrape. Everyone's to *breathe* quietly until Georgina and I open the doors. When that happens, I want you to shout 'Surprise!' at the very top of your lungs."

"If we're that quiet, how's Sam supposed to know we're here?" one of Sam's elderly great-aunts, Cassandra Jeffords, asked testily.

With exaggerated patience, as if she were a primary-grade teacher addressing a disruptive pupil, Halette explained that he'd probably head straight for the shower when he came in, as he had a dinner engagement with Dacinda. "We'll make some sort of noise...possibly move a piece of furniture," she suggested. "Surprise him when he comes downstairs . . . wrapped in a towel . . . to investigate."

Everyone laughed at the mental image her words evoked. Though it dropped to an obedient murmur, it wasn't long before the noise level in the room had reintensified. Suddenly, "Here he comes!" Sallie warned in an exaggerated stage whisper, scuttling into the room and easing the double doors completely shut behind her. "He's just pullin' into the drive."

Abandoning Lizzie, Shelby wedged herself between Dacinda and Marcie for a better view. For her part, Marcie was wired with anticipation. She couldn't wait to see the look of astonishment on Sam's face. It's going to be downright comical, she thought—especially when he realizes I've come all the way from New York to watch his sisters put one over on him.

A moment later, the Jeep's door slammed. Sam's footsteps could be heard on the porch. "Did you relock the front door?" Halette whispered anxiously, violating her own instructions.

Sallie nodded. "What do you take me for... an idiot?" she mouthed.

As Halette had predicted, after unlocking the front door, Sam threw his keys down on the hall table and went straight upstairs. The guests exchanged surprised looks a moment later when the sound of conversation, rather than that of a shower running, drifted back down to them.

"Either he's talkin' to himself or he's turned on the radio," one of Sam's cousins surmised under his breath. "We'll have to make some real noise to get his attention."

Upstairs, Sam was staring at Carolyn in consternation. "What the hell are you doing here, dressed like that?" he demanded, rephrasing his original question.

Arranged on his bed in a suggestive pose worthy of a well-known mail-order catalog that featured sexy lingerie, Carolyn wore a red lace peignoir, matching bra and bikini panties. Though her lower lip quivered at his accusing tone, she slithered off his rumpled spread and crossed the space between them. "Happy birthday, darlin'," she whispered, twining her arms about his neck.

Firmly he disengaged himself. "I want to know how you got in," he repeated. "Did you break a window? Or..."

"What does it matter, honey lamb? I came to celebrate with you. If you don't like my outfit, I can always take it off."

Sam was horrified. "Don't you dare! Not unless it's to change clothes in the bathroom so you can go home!"

As he spoke, several of the party guests cooperated to push his desk a few feet across the uncarpeted wood floor of his office. The electrifying sound their efforts produced riveted Sam's attention. "There's somebody in the house!" he exclaimed, lowering his voice. "Stay here. I'm going to investigate."

"If it's a criminal, I want to be with you." Her manner oddly reluctant despite her protest, Carolyn insisted on following him.

Focused as he was on the fact that an intruder might have broken into the house with the intent of robbing him, Sam didn't think of calling the police. Nor did Carolyn suggest it. He couldn't guess that she saw no reason to. Or that her primary emotion might not be fear, but a natural tendency to cringe at anticipated humiliation.

His footsteps as soundless as he could make them on the creaky, two-hundred-year-old treads, Sam reached the bottom of the stairs with Carolyn tiptoeing after him. Though he hadn't noticed it when he'd come in, because of his haste to shower and change clothes for his date with Dacinda, someone had shut the double doors to his office. He was positive he'd left them open. Had some rag of a publication sent one of its minions to pirate his upcoming strip? Or was a burglar attempting to rifle the safe he'd installed a few months earlier?

Casting wildly about for some sort of weapon, he snatched up the only object that caught his eye—a heavy clay flowerpot containing a thoroughly neglected dieffen-bachia. If necessary, he could use the pot to knock the cul-prit off balance. Ludicrous in her red lace getup, Carolyn continued to hover one step behind him. If physical harm threatened, apparently, she planned to use him as a shield. A hell of a birthday this is turning out to be, he thought.

"Okay…whoever you are," he said, raising his voice to a menacing growl and holding his dieffenbachia at the ready. "Come out and show yourself!"

In Sam's office, the party guests had crowded close to the double doors. They were poised and ready to let loose a spine-tingling yell.

At Halette's signal, she and Georgina flung the doors open wide. "Surprise!" everyone shouted at full banshee register.

A moment later, silence reigned as every man, woman and child present gaped at him and Carolyn. Sam froze like a deer caught in a Mack truck's headlights. To his aston-ishment, *Marcie* was there, along with his mother, sisters and almost everyone he knew in Charleston. Though they flickered back and forth from Carolyn's face to his, all eyes seemed focused on her state of undress. Belatedly he real-ized how ridiculous and guilty the two of them must look. What in God's name had possessed her to pull such a crazy stunt? More to the point, what must his friends and loved ones think of him?

"This isn't…what it seems," he stammered, groping for some form of damage control.

At his words, Carolyn burst into tears.

"We…uh, didn't realize…" Georgina whispered, her face flushed with what appeared to be genuine embarrass-ment and regret.

Partially freed from his temporary paralysis at her words, Sam set the dieffenbachia down at his feet and reached into his coat closet for a somewhat threadbare tan raincoat. "Go upstairs and get dressed," he said curtly, draping it around Carolyn's shoulders. "That's an order."

Her tears intensifying to a flood, she complied.

The exchange gave impetus to Marcie, too. A bundle of freewheeling emotions thanks to the physical changes being wrought in her by pregnancy, she felt as if the bottom had dropped out of her world. If Carolyn had the run of Sam's house in her negligee, there could be only one reason. Believing her safely in New York, they'd arranged to share a birthday tryst. The fact that he'd turned on her didn't excuse it.

A hothead by temperament, though she did her best to struggle for self-control, she was hurt, disillusioned and furious. To make matters worse, infidelity was an extremely touchy subject with her. Just Shelby's age when she'd learned her father had cheated on her mother, she'd vowed never to become the victim of that particular sort of treatment. The memory of that vow had colored her perception the night of their breakup, when Sam had danced with another brunette at the awards banquet. Now it was doing so again.

Shaking off Dacinda's hand, she pushed past Sam without a word. A moment later, the screen door was banging shut behind her.

"Marcie, wait!" he shouted, starting after her. "If you'll just hear me out . . ."

Georgina appeared to give herself a mental shake. She caught him firmly by the arm. "Sam, I'm so sorry," she whispered. "We had no idea . . ."

"God, no," Halette echoed, unobtrusively blocking his exit on the other side. "How could we? It was *awful*."

As she watched her best friend's mother and Halette Mills smother Sam's impulse to go after Marcie, Shelby rolled her eyes.

Though Marcie had come with Dacinda, and didn't have a rental car at her disposal, the latter's house was just a few blocks away. Thank heaven you didn't bother to unpack, she congratulated herself as she quickened her pace in order to put even greater distance between herself and the man she was convinced had broken her heart. She'd call a cab from Dacinda's, she decided. Take the next plane out of Charleston no matter what its destination.

So far, Sam hadn't bothered to follow her. Though she didn't want any trumped-up apologies from him, the fact that he'd let her go without the slightest effort to set things straight made her angrier still. What a fool he looked, holding up that stupid plant as if he could use it to defend himself! she thought disparagingly. As for Carolyn, her choice in peignoirs made her look like a hooker.

The two of them deserved each other. She was better off without him . . . even if she was having his baby. As the full force of what had happened hit her, she dissolved in tears.

At Sam's house, the embarrassed party guests were murmuring apologies and taking their leave. When the last of them had gone, Carolyn reappeared in shorts and a T-shirt, clutching her negligee and red lace underthings in a shopping bag. Giving Halette and Georgina a speaking look though she didn't actually say anything to them, she strode out the door.

Sam scarcely noticed. Pacing his office, which still contained the trappings of his aborted birthday party, he'd begun to work up quite a head of steam. By now, most of it was directed at Marcie. He loved her, damn it. And he was worthy of her trust. Though admittedly it had looked bad, she'd done him a grave disservice to believe him so faithless.

Attempting to reason with him, Dacinda gave up in manifest frustration. "C'mon, Shelby," she said with a little shake of her head. "We may as well go home and have a bite to eat."

They arrived in time to see Marcie's cab pull up. In response to the driver's honk, Marcie herself emerged a moment later, toting her carry-on bag.

"No! She can't leave!" Shelby cried. Jumping out of the station wagon, she ran forward and blocked Marcie's path. "Sam loves you, no matter how it looks," she insisted, attempting to wrest Marcie's bag from her grip. "Don't you know *anything?*"

As the cabbie watched and waited, Dacinda joined them. "Shelby's right," she echoed reprovingly though she forced the girl to unhand Marcie's luggage. "I daresay I know Sam as well as anyone. And he's been the happiest I've seen him in quite some time since the two of you got back together. There's bound to be a rational explanation for what occurred."

Marcie was in no mood to listen. If Sam cares so much, where is he? she retorted silently. Comforting Carolyn, I'll bet. Thank heaven she hadn't told Dacinda about the baby.

"Sorry. But I'm out of here," she said, causing Shelby to mutter rebelliously. "I put up with a lot from Sam during our first go-round. I don't plan to do it again."

By the time Sam had regained sufficient perspective to head for his mother's house, Marcie was gone. On learning she'd taken a cab to the airport, he decided not to follow her, though Shelby begged him to do so. He was innocent of wrongdoing. Unless Marcie came to that conclusion without any help from him, they wouldn't have much of a future together.

"Sorry, Shel," he said, his heart like a lump of granite in his chest as he gave the distraught child a hug. "But Marcie's a big girl. She's old enough to make her own decisions."

Dacinda shot him an incredulous look. "Not necessarily. You're older than she is . . . thirty-eight as of this mornin' if I remember correctly. And you're not doin' too well yourself."

Sam refused to take offense. Or argue with her. "I know you care, Mom," he admitted. "But I want you to stay out of this. Either Marcie trusts me. Or she doesn't. It's that simple."

Dacinda nodded her agreement with obvious reluctance. "I can't imagine what Carolyn was doin' there, dressed like that," she mused, her frown lines deepening slightly. "She must have known about the party. I wonder what could have possessed her to pull such a crazy stunt?"

Given the jangled state of his emotions, Sam answered with relative gentleness. "I'll be damned if I know. I sure as hell didn't encourage her."

"Maybe I ought to have a little talk with your sisters."

He didn't catch her implication, though Shelby obviously did. Just then a jet passed overhead, gaining altitude. Glancing skyward, he wondered if Marcie was on it. Determined to wait her out, for months, if necessary, he needed comforting. "C'mon, Shel," he said with a sigh. "Let's go get some ice cream."

For the first time ever, Shelby refused him. "You and Marcie are both incredibly dumb," she told him in disgust, earning a reprimand from Dacinda.

Chapter Eleven

As she holed up in her New York apartment, amid the boxes and packing materials she'd begun to accumulate, and tried to acquit herself honorably during her final two months at *Zoom*, Marcie's anguish was acute. She'd do something different for a living come October, that much was certain. But what? And where? Sam's baby was growing inside her body. She needed someplace suited to raising a child, preferably one where she wouldn't have to see its father any oftener than necessary, work that would allow her to spend time with her little one. She began to think about taking an exploratory trip to the Pacific Northwest.

A feeling of bleakness beyond anything she'd ever experienced had set in when Sam hadn't called. Her imagination running wild, she'd pictured scene after scene of him romancing Carolyn. Of course by now, he'd probably dumped the idiot brunette, as well. Clearly, fidelity wasn't his strong suit.

To her chagrin, she continued to feel deep love for him and have second thoughts about her own behavior. Suppose he's innocent and I've completely misjudged him, she thought one rainy evening as she curled up alone in front of her television set. What if there was a reasonable explanation for Carolyn hanging out in his house in her negligee when he had every reason to believe I was in New York?

Each time she posed those questions, she couldn't seem to help asking herself another one. If Sam wasn't guilty of cheating, why hadn't he contacted her? She couldn't think of a satisfactory reason. Meanwhile, morning bouts of nausea that forced her to eat breakfast twice in order to start the workday with something in her stomach, and the incontrovertible changes of pregnancy did nothing to alleviate her distress. In a fit of desperation that was secretly aimed at prodding Sam into getting in touch with her, she asked Bob Richmond to activate their final divorce proceedings.

As he sleepwalked through the remaining days and nights of the loggerhead turtle nesting season, Sam kept hoping to hear from her. She knew his address, damn it. Both his phone numbers. One of these days, he believed, she'd break down and call.

Sometimes in the wee hours, when he returned to his Edisto cottage after a night spent patrolling the beach, he fantasized how her apology would go. Tormented with second thoughts about her own behavior, she wouldn't ask him to explain Carolyn's presence. Instead, she'd admit, over and over, how sorry she was—how much she loved and trusted him. Safe in his arms, she'd shudder to think they'd almost done it again—played out the same terrible scenario of alienation and loneliness twice over. Not a letter came, not a postcard. Though he stared at it, willing it to ring, the phone stayed stubbornly silent.

In addition to the pain Marcie's defection had caused, something else was bothering him. Following his disastrous birthday party and Marcie's hasty departure, both he and Shelby had been down in the dumps. Spiriting her off to the beach in the hope of cheering her up and giving Glenn and Dacinda a little elbow room, he'd broken down and told her about his petition to begin adoption proceedings in her case.

"My lawyer and I spoke to the judge about this...probably a month ago," he'd said. "She hasn't given us an answer yet. Before we go any further, I was wondering how..."

Anticipating the rest of his question, Shelby had given him a fierce hug. "Oh, Sam, please...*yes!*" she'd whispered.

Though it undeniably had warmed his heart, her elation had quickly become something of a reproach to him. At a meeting in Charleston the next day, Jerry Bartholomew had reminded him of his quasi-single status and the judge's ultratraditional outlook, and warned him not to expect too much. Given her record in such matters, she might not allow him to petition for Shelby's custody. What if the judge says no, and sends Shelby off, as a foster child, to live with strangers? he'd asked himself. After getting her hopes up, I'll feel like a barbarian. Gloomy and out of sorts with himself, he'd left the lawyer's office wishing he'd held his tongue.

Now, as he labored in Joe Bain's front yard, helping the elderly crabber paint fresh creosote on his wooden traps, he was edgy, wondering if the phone would ring. He didn't expect Marcie to call. In truth, he'd all but given up on her. Besides, he knew she wouldn't phone him at Joe's.

Rather, it was Jerry he half dreaded would be on the other end of the line. It was a Friday, and the adoption judge usually rendered her decisions at the end of the week.

Aware they could expect one from her at any moment, he'd somewhat nervously left Joe's number with the lawyer's secretary.

Popping open a beer and taking a swig to ease the dry feeling in his throat, Sam nearly jumped a foot when the phone inside Joe's modest cottage shrilled. In response to its summons, the old crabber got up slowly, favoring his arthritic joints.

"Could be the call you're waitin' for," he speculated, giving his tobacco quid a chomp.

A minute later, Joe was motioning to him from the cottage's open doorway, the receiver of his outdated telephone dangling from one gnarled hand. "Jerry Bartholomew callin' from Charleston," he said, raising one grizzled brow like a question mark.

The moment Sam heard the lawyer's voice, he guessed the news wasn't good. "The judge isn't going to give me a chance, is she?" he asked bitterly, trying to blunt the overwhelming rush of disappointment he felt.

He could almost see the lawyer shaking his head. "'Fraid not, old buddy," Jerry answered regretfully. "It's your single status, like we feared. You might as well know...she's talking about transferring the girl to foster care until a permanent placement can be arranged."

Sam swore.

"I don't suppose Dacinda..." Jerry asked.

Before Glenn, Sam wouldn't have hesitated to predict that his mother would take the girl. Now that she was about to remarry and begin a new life with her retired navy officer turned editor, he didn't know what she'd do. Or whether he had any right to ask her for further assistance with the little girl he loved. After all the years Dacinda had spent totally focused on work, with only a superficial personal life, he supposed, it would be unfair to saddle her with a ten-year-old. If only he and Marcie...

"I don't honestly know, Jer," he admitted, aware his voice had a hollow ring.

For several seconds the line hummed empty of conversation. The lawyer's silence gave Sam an apprehensive, sinking feeling. "The business about Shelby... It's not the only reason you called, is it?" he asked.

Jerry Bartholomew's sigh seemed to arise from some deep, hollow place. "No, it isn't, Sam. I, uh, got a letter from your wife's attorney in this morning's mail. She's asking for a quick dissolution."

Pain shot through Sam's gut. It was all he could do to keep from clutching at his stomach. He couldn't have Marcie and he couldn't have Shel. Everything he tried to do turned to ashes. Swearing and then apologizing to Jerry Bartholomew for his use of bad language, he put down the phone.

"You want another beer?" Joe asked sympathetically.

For the first time in a long while, Sam realized, he was on the verge of tears. "Hell, I want a couple," he said, furious at the break in his voice.

"You got 'em."

Chugalugging two more beers as he ranted to Joe about all the injustice in the world, Sam returned to his own cottage on foot in the late-afternoon heat, leaving his Jeep parked beneath one of the crabber's shade trees. His speech and thinking were somewhat impaired as he dialed Dacinda's number and poured out his tale of woe.

He could almost hear her sharp intake of breath at the double-barreled tragedy that was unfolding. "Sam, darlin'... I'm so sorry!" she exclaimed. "What can I do?"

Take Shelby, he wanted to reply. But he couldn't make himself do it.

Agreeing with him that the judge's decision was shortsighted and offering what comfort she could, Sam's mother begged him not to tell the girl or anyone else about its particulars until they could come up with an alternate plan. "It would only cause her to worry," she insisted. "My heart tells me we can do *somethin'* to put things right."

Thanks to Georgina's presence in Dacinda's drawing room, where she'd been arguing with her mother when Sam called, it wasn't long before the story spread. That very night, Shelby was due to sleep over with Georgina's daughter, Lizzie, and the girls' get-together proceeded on schedule. Though Georgina kept her word to Dacinda and didn't say anything directly to Shelby about what she knew, she managed to do the damage she'd forsworn anyway. Sneaking downstairs for cookies and cans of soda after Lizzie's parents thought them safely in bed, the girls overheard Georgina telling her husband, Jim, what had occurred.

Shelby's face went white at the news that Sam wouldn't be allowed to adopt her. She was equally stricken to learn Marcie was divorcing him.

Her eyes huge with compassion, Lizzie dragged her friend back upstairs. "What do you suppose will happen?" she asked worriedly when they were once again huddled in the privacy of her beribboned and ruffled bedroom. "Will you have to go and live with strangers, do you suppose?"

Shelby didn't tell Lizzie. But a plan was already forming in her head. Determined to have Sam for her new dad and Marcie for her mother, she waited until Monday when Dacinda was occupied at the *Gazette* and Salome had gone out to do the week's marketing, before shifting it into gear. After copying Marcie's New York phone number from Dacinda's address book and filching some cash and one of Dacinda's less frequently used credit cards from a desk drawer in the latter's study, she picked up the phone and dialed one of the major airlines' toll-free numbers.

"This is Dacinda Jeffords," she said in her most grown-up voice when an operator answered. "I'd like a round-trip ticket to New York for this afternoon . . . for my daughter. There's been a death in her father's family. She'll be traveling to meet him." The telephone ticket clerk didn't seem to sense anything was amiss. Quoting a price that sent Shelby's eyebrows and guilt quotient rocketing through the roof, she asked for a name, address and credit-card number.

By the time she put down the receiver, Shelby had a departure time and seat assignment. All she lacked was gate information. She could get that at the airport. Though she was frightened, both of traveling alone and of the gravity of her transgression, she'd had the presence of mind to pack a bag so the airline stewardesses wouldn't get suspicious. Time to call a cab before Salome gets back and catches me, she thought.

Salome didn't report the girl missing until it was almost dinnertime, believing her to be playing at Lizzie's house. Instantly worried, Dacinda called Georgina and then Sam. Had Shelby found out about the judge's decision? It was possible she'd run away. Nobody seemed to know where she was.

As they spoke, Shelby was deplaning in New York amid a crowd of hurrying adults. The sky was overcast, heavy with rain clouds. It looked much cooler outside than it had been in Charleston.

With plenty of time enroute to contemplate what she'd done, Shelby had become more and more troubled by her own audacity. Suppose Marcie was out of town on an assignment? What would she do? From what she'd heard people say, she didn't think it would safe to take a cab to Marcie's apartment building and wait for her.

Aware one of the uniformed airline officials had noticed her and was eyeing her speculatively, she hurried up to a kindly looking elderly man and threw her arms around him.

"Well, hello, young lady!" he said with a smile though he was obviously startled. "Should I know you?"

Despite the manners Dacinda had begun drilling into her, Shelby didn't answer him. Out of the corner of her eye she saw that the official had glanced away. Clutching her overnight bag, she scooted for the nearest telephone.

Marcie was just returning home from work. As she inserted her key in her front-door lock, the phone began to ring. Had Sam finally called her? Fumbling in her eagerness, she raced to pick up the receiver. "Hello?" she answered breathlessly.

The voice on the other end of the line caused her brows to lift. "Hi, Marcie," it said. "This is Shelby. I, um, ran away from home. Could you please come pick me up at La Guardia Airport?"

A short time later, Marcie was bundling a grateful Shelby into her car and merging with rush-hour traffic. "What's going on?" she asked, darting the girl an incredulous glance. "Dacinda must be worried sick...."

Shelby swallowed. "Could we wait to talk until we get to your apartment?"

About to insist they discuss things immediately, Marcie relented as caught a suspicious glint of tears beneath Shelby's pale lashes. What the girl needed was a hug, not recriminations. "All right," she agreed, reaching over to pat Shelby's hand. "But then you've got to come clean. I'm going to want the whole story."

Forty-five minutes later, after they'd twice been stalled in traffic, Shelby was huddled at Marcie's kitchen table as Marcie put on the kettle for hot chocolate. Still mum about her motives for the stunt she'd pulled, she leapt to her feet when Marcie lifted the receiver of her kitchen phone and began to dial Dacinda's number.

"*Please,* Marcie," she begged. "Don't call yet. Let me tell you what happened first."

By now, Marcie guessed, both her mother-in-law and Sam must be frantic. They'd probably called the police. Yet again she hesitated. She couldn't help wondering why Shelby had run away. And what had caused the girl to seek refuge with her.

"Okay," she conceded, replacing the receiver and stirring boiling water into two mugs containing powdered hot chocolate mix. "*Start talking.*"

Speaking in something of a monotone, Shelby recounted the discussion that had taken place in Georgina Herndon's living room three days before. According to Sam's sister, she said, his petition to begin proceedings to adopt her had been rejected. Meanwhile, Dacinda was getting married. She, Shelby, would be shunted off to a foster home. The judge would see to it.

"It's not fair," she said. "I'll be sent to live with strangers...all because you and Sam aren't planning to stay married. Why did you have to leave Charleston without listening to him? I know he could have explained...."

Though she burned with indignation to think Shelby might lose what semblance of family she had left, Marcie hardened her heart when her rejection of Sam was mentioned. "What did you expect me to do?" she shot back defensively, forgetting she was dealing with a child. "You saw what was going on!"

Shelby took a sip of her hot chocolate. "I know what I saw," she answered. "But I don't think it was real. Sam doesn't even *like* Carolyn Deane. Most of the time, he acts like she's got something contagious."

Marcie's eyes narrowed. "If that's true, what was she doing in his house...in a red lace negligee?"

Munching on one of the cookies Marcie had arranged on a plate for her in lieu of rustling up some dinner, Shelby took her time about answering. "I think what happened the afternoon of the party was actually a plot by Mrs. Herndon and Mrs. Mills to make you go away so Carolyn could have Sam," she said at last. "I can't prove it. But Dacinda thinks so, too. I can tell. She's pretty mad at them."

Having spent more time than she cared to admit stewing over the question of Sam's guilt or innocence, Marcie was forced to acknowledge that Shelby's words had the ring of truth. In her opinion, Halette Mills and Georgina Herndon were sufficiently headstrong, mean-spirited and juvenile that they'd attempt to break up their brother's marriage in just such a fashion if it suited them. No doubt her acceptance of Shelby's story—not to mention her own foolishness for swallowing the illusion Sam's sisters had created, hook, line and sinker—was written all over her face.

Shelby had the wisdom not to rub her nose in it. Nevertheless, Marcie was painfully aware the girl thought she should have trusted Sam. If I fail at this, my second chance to recognize and believe the truth, I deserve to lose him, she thought. And fall irretrievably low in Shelby's regard.

At some point, she realized, the youngster's good opinion had begun to matter a great deal to her. Sam's, of course, meant the earth. The question was, would he take her back? From deep within, an answer surfaced. Sam loved her. But he wasn't going to beg for her trust. He was waiting for her to offer it. After so much confusion and misery, her certainty that she'd finally read the situation right was like manna to her soul.

Nobody had to hit her over the head to make her realize that Shelby was hardly an unbiased observer. The girl had sought her out in New York because she wanted to ease Sam's unhappiness, true. But she also wanted a family.

And she wanted Sam for her father. She'd figured out that, if he and Marcie reconciled, she'd get her wish.

"If I can get Sam to take me back, do you think you could stand having me for a mom, Shelby?" she asked.

Abruptly the ten-year-old's tough, worldly wise facade crumbled. "Oh, *yes,*" she whispered tearfully, coming around the table to nestle in Marcie's arms.

A good bit of hugging was exchanged before they phoned Dacinda. In addition, Marcie came up with a bright idea. Setting her mother-in-law's mind at ease, she wrung a promise from her not to tell Sam his errant young protégée's whereabouts. "I know he'll worry if you don't," she admitted. "But it won't be for long. Shelby and I are flying back to Charleston in the morning. He's going to get the surprise party he missed."

"You mean...?" Dacinda sounded as if she could hardly believe her ears.

"That's right," Marcie exulted. "There'll be one guest of honor—Sam. And two hostesses, namely myself and Shelby. That's it. In case you're wondering, I plan to apologize. And promise to love and trust him all my days."

Her voice weak with relief, Dacinda gave the scheme her unqualified approval. "I'll leave the spare key under the mat," she said. "And get Sam to show up at the house somehow. Just tell me what time you want him to appear."

Marcie made two subsequent phone calls that evening—the first to Glenn and the second to the airlines. Aware Dacinda probably was trying to reach Glenn, too, she kept her request brief. "I need emergency leave...to fly back down to Charleston and save my marriage," she said.

"Well, it's about time!" His voice gruff with pleasure, Dacinda's husband-to-be urged her to take all she wanted.

* * *

Arriving in South Carolina late the following morning, Marcie and Shelby set to work cleaning Sam's house and making a fabulous feast of crab imperial. They also baked his favorite chocolate cake. By late afternoon, the time he was expected back to meet with the private detective Dacinda supposedly had hired to find Shelby, they were ready for him.

The instant Sam opened his front door, he sensed somebody was in the house. Oh, no, he thought. I hope to hell it isn't Carolyn again. I'd almost prefer the burglar I thought was robbing me on my birthday.

A moment later, it occurred to him that his bachelor digs looked uncommonly neat. Simultaneously his olfactory nerve announced that something smelled awfully good. Before he could puzzle over the cleanliness of his front hall, or place the spicy aroma that was teasing his nostrils, a slight sound issued from the kitchen.

It was déjà vu. Cautiously, half expecting a pie to hit him in the face or Carolyn to reappear in her negligee, he pushed the door open.

"Surprise!" Marcie and Shelby shouted, jumping out of the pantry in unison.

Dumbfounded, Sam wasn't sure whether to feel relief, pleasure or irritation. Marcie's lawyer *had* sent him the divorce papers at her behest, hadn't he? So what was she doing here, in the enemy camp? As for Shelby, she'd caused him no end of worry. He hoped her running away hadn't been some kind of dreadful practical joke—one in which, unthinkably, he was the fall guy and Dacinda and Marcie were the perpetrators.

"So... there you are, Shelby. I'm waiting for an explanation," he said, folding his arms across his chest and staring at his would-be daughter though he kept Marcie firmly fixed in his peripheral vision, lest she should disappear.

Throwing herself at him in a little rush, Shelby flung her arms around him. Contritely, but in a faintly wheedling tone that suggested she was a past master at talking her way out of trouble, she apologized for worrying him. "But you know, Sam...if you and Marcie hadn't let Mrs. Herndon and Mrs. Mills split you up that way," she pointed out, "I wouldn't have had to go to New York and fix things."

No stranger to the girl's tactics, Sam shot Marcie a look. "New York! Is that true?"

"She called me from La Guardia yesterday evening, and asked me to pick her up."

"Incredible." He was silent a moment. "What's this she's saying about Halette and Georgina?"

Sam got the same explanation Marcie had received the night before. Compelled to agree it was probably valid, he wanted to wring his sisters' necks. He decided they could wait. Right now, he had more important business.

"Plane tickets are expensive. How did you manage to pay for yours, Shel?" he asked. "I didn't realize your allowance was that generous."

The girl had the presence of mind to look abashed. Again Marcie answered for her. "She 'borrowed' Dacinda's credit card. I have a feeling she'll be paying off the debt for the next couple of years. That is, unless I agree to go halves with her. Running away was wrong—" she gave Shelby a severe look "—but, the fact is, I benefitted."

Sam thought he knew what was coming. God knew he'd waited for it long enough. "How's that?" he asked, his eyes getting their lazy look.

"She managed to convince me I'd behaved like an idiot by not trusting you. If you'll take me back, I promise...it'll never happen again."

The six feet or so of kitchen that separated them felt like the Grand Canyon to Marcie as Sam considered her plea.

Part of him wanted to stay angry with her, though he'd been more sad than seething. She'd put him through hell, hadn't she, when none of what had transpired had been his fault? Another part argued that she'd come to her senses without any tangible proof he hadn't been cheating on her. Nobody had pressured her to believe Shelby. Besides— whatever she'd done—there'd never been any doubt he'd forgive her.

With a little shake of his head that told how much he loved Marcie, he opened his arms. The three-way hug that resulted seemed to last forever. Ultimately they had to let go of each other. The crab imperial, asparagus au gratin and corn fritters Marcie and Shelby had worked so hard to make would have been all dried-out otherwise. Landing a kiss on Marcie's mouth that was sweetened by the brief, clandestine insertion of his tongue, Sam served notice that they'd have their own private reunion.

It was family time first. Over supper, her mouth full of crab, which she claimed to love even more than pizza, Shelby declared that now Sam could adopt her. She and Marcie had it all worked out.

"Is that so?" Sam asked, looking at Marcie with love.

They'd talked it over, of course, before his disastrous birthday party. But they hadn't come to any hard and fast conclusions then. Now she knew with the deepest kind of knowing it was exactly the right thing to do. "It's true. Shelby recruited me," she confirmed, her heart full with the other, parenthood-related news she hadn't told him yet.

Sam rolled his eyes at the irrepressible ten-year-old. "Little Miss Fix-it, aren't you?" he teased. "Maybe we ought to reconsider. I'm beginning to think we had no idea what we'd be getting ourselves into with you."

Though Shelby was riding high at the prospect of helping create a family with them, she didn't rule the evening altogether. Once the dishes were washed and put away, Sam announced they were taking her back to Dacinda's.

"What for? Why can't I stay here if I'm going to be your kid?" she protested.

Sam and Marcie exchanged a look.

Knowledgeable beyond her years when it came to the quirks of adults, Shelby made a face. "Oh, I get it," she groaned. "Mush stuff."

In the Jeep on the way back to his house from Dacinda's, Sam could barely see to drive. The weeks since his aborted birthday party had been long, lonely ones for both of them. He and Marcie couldn't seem to stop kissing, or keep their hands off each other. The moment they were inside his front door, Sam made a grab for her. Articles of clothing fell to the floor one after another as they mounted the stairs to his room.

It would be *their* room. Their life. At the thought of all the love they'd make, the ever more intimate and tender life they'd build together, Marcie shed her last qualm about the profound changes she was making. That night, her culmination was the most powerful yet.

So was Sam's. Afterward, as they drifted lazily in their contentment, Marcie told him about the baby. Ecstatic, though at first he could hardly believe she was serious, Sam characteristically saw the humor in the situation. "Ten to one, it'll be a girl," he asserted, contemplating future cartoons. "I'll be surrounded by women."

"You *like* women," Marcie reminded him.

He grinned. "You're right." A moment later, his face took on a thoughtful, almost contemplative expression. "Red, little Red and Shelby Ann Jeffords, stunt artist par excellence," he said. "Something tells me it's going to be an interesting combination."

Epilogue

May, 1995

It was a sunny day, still breezy in the early-morning hours but with the promise of a sweltering afternoon to come. As Marcie rocked two-month-old Lauren Elizabeth Jeffords on the piazza of Sam's renovated single house, he and their older daughter, Shelby Ann, cooed lovingly at the baby. Though Lauren hadn't exactly smiled yet, she seemed on the verge of doing so at any moment as her eyes followed the music-box teddy bear Shelby was bobbing up and down for her inspection.

A lot had happened in the eleven months since the tiny, redheaded girl baby had been conceived—on the beach at Edisto, if Sam was to be believed. Shelby's adoption had become final two months earlier. In addition, Marcie had started outlining her book and begun her postgraduate studies. During the same period, Sam's strip, which tended to lag behind his life experiences by a month or so, had evolved to portray the more hilarious moments of fatherhood.

Beside Marcie on the swing, that morning's edition of the *Gazette* lay folded open to his latest effort. Characteristically droll, it depicted a pregnant woman and her husband, who had changed into the required hospital garb to go into the labor and delivery rooms together. For some reason—a misguided attempt to keep the birth process sterile, perhaps?—the nervous, first-time dad had emulated his wife in stripping to the skin beneath his hospital gown.

In the final frame, a nurse laughed and shook her head as the couple emerged from the dressing room. "You can put your clothes back on beneath your gown, sir," she told the father-to-be gently. "You're not having the baby. Your *wife* is. You're just the cheering section."

*　*　*　*　*

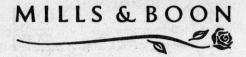

MILLS & BOON

January's Romances

Each month you can choose from a wide variety of romance with Mills & Boon. Below are the new titles to look out for in January.

THE FATHERHOOD AFFAIR	Emma Darcy
AN UNFORGETTABLE MAN	Penny Jordan
TWO'S COMPANY	Carole Mortimer
FALLEN HERO	Catherine George
AN INDECENT PROPOSAL	Sandra Marton
THE MARRIAGE BUSINESS	Jessica Steele
A FORBIDDEN SEDUCTION	Sara Wood
TERMS OF POSSESSION	Elizabeth Power
SWEET LIES	Catherine O'Connor
HEARTLESS ABDUCTION	Angela Wells
STOLEN FEELINGS	Margaret Mayo
THE OTHER MAN	Karen van der Zee
PROMISE OF PARADISE	Rosemary Hammond
BEYOND RICHES	Catherine Leigh
THE BAD PENNY	Susan Fox
WIFE-TO-BE	Jessica Hart

Available from WH Smith, John Menzies, Volume One, Forbuoys, Martins, Woolworths, Tesco, Asda, Safeway and other paperback stockists.

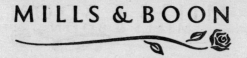

MILLS & BOON

February's Romances

Each month you can choose from a wide variety of romance with Mills & Boon. Below are the new titles to look out for in February.

ANGRY DESIRE	Charlotte Lamb
THE VALENTINE CHILD	Jacqueline Baird
THE UNFAITHFUL WIFE	Lynne Graham
A KISS TO REMEMBER	Miranda Lee
GUARDIAN GROOM	Sandra Marton
PRIVATE DANCER	Eva Rutland
THE MARRIAGE SOLUTION	Helen Brooks
SECOND HONEYMOON	Sandra Field
MARRIAGE VOWS	Rosalie Ash
THE WEDDING DECEPTION	Kay Thorpe
THE HERO TRAP	Rosemary Badger
FORSAKING ALL OTHERS	Susanne McCarthy
RELENTLESS SEDUCTION	Kim Lawrence
PILLOW TALK	Rebecca King
EVERY WOMAN'S DREAM	Bethany Campbell
A BRIDE FOR RANSOM	Renee Roszel

MILLS & BOON

Stories of love you'll treasure forever...

Popular Australian author Miranda Lee brings you a
brand new trilogy within the Romance line–
Affairs to Remember.

Based around a special affair of a lifetime, each
book is packed full of sensuality with some
unusual features and twists along the way!

This is Miranda Lee at her very best.

Look out for:

A Kiss To Remember in February '96
A Weekend To Remember in March '96
A Woman To Remember in April '96

MILLS & BOON

Don't miss our great new series within the Romance line...

Landon's Legacy

One book a month focusing on each of the four members of the Landon family—three brothers and one sister—and the effect the death of their father has on their lives.

You won't want to miss any of these involving, passionate stories all written by Sandra Marton.

Look out for:

An Indecent Proposal in January '96
Guardian Groom in February '96
Hollywood Wedding in March '96
Spring Bride in April '96

Cade, Grant, Zach and Kyra Landon—four people who find love and marriage as a result of their legacy.